One-on-One

I can hoop. I can definitely hoop. I ain't jamming but I'm scamming. You may look great but you will look late. You got the ball against me and you blink and all you got left is the stink because I got the ball and gone. I played one-on-one with my shadow and my shadow couldn't keep up. But that's about all I do, which is now a problem since my dad is living in the city and dropping by all the time.

"Is that all you do?" he asked. "Play basketball?"

"I watch television," I said.

ALSO BY WALTER DEAN MYERS

Scorpions

The Righteous Revenge of Artemis Bonner

Now Is Your Time!
The African-American Struggle for Freedom

Brown Angels
An Album of Pictures and Verse

Glorious Angels
A Celebration of Children

Angel to Angel
A Mother's Gift of Love

WALTER DEAN MYERS

THE MOUSE RAP

HarperTrophy®
A Division of HarperCollinsPublishers

Harper Trophy® is a registered trademark of HarperCollins Publishers Inc.

The Mouse Rap

Typography by Joyce Hopkins

Library of Congress Cataloging-in-Publication Data
Myers, Walter Dean, date
   The mouse rap / by Walter Dean Myers.
      p.   cm.
   Summary: During an eventful summer in Harlem, fourteen-year-old Mouse and his friends fall
in and out of love and search for a hidden treasure from the days of Al Capone.
   ISBN 0-06-024343-0. — ISBN 0-06-024344-9 (lib. bdg.)
   ISBN 0-06-440356-4 (pbk.)
   [1. Harlem (New York, N.Y.)—Fiction.   2. Afro-Americans—Fiction.
3. Buried treasure—Fiction.]   I. Title.
PZ7.M992Mou   1990   89-36419
[Fic]—dc20   CIP
                                                                                          AC

First Harper Trophy edition, 1992.

Visit us on the World Wide Web!
http://www.harperchildrens.com

To Harriett Brown,
who has contibuted so much
to the cause of children's literature

Ka-phoomp! Ka-phoomp! Da Doom Da Dooom!
Ka-phoomp! Ka-phoomp! Da Doom Da Dooom!
You can call me Mouse, 'cause that's my tag
I'm into it all, everything's my bag
You know I can run, you know I can hoop
I can do it alone, or in a group
My ace is Styx, he'll always do
Add Bev and Sheri, and you got my crew
My tag is Mouse, and it'll never fail
And just like a mouse I got me a tale
Ka-phoomp! Ka-phoomp! Da Doom Da Dooom!
Ka-phoomp! Ka-phoomp! Da Doom Da Dooom!

☆

"I should have known something was up," I
said as Styx and I left the library.

3

"Yo, Mouse, you got to get it off your mind."

"Get it off my mind? How would you like to come home and find some dude making eyes at your mother?"

"He's not some dude. He's your father."

"You remember the time I spent the weekend at your house?"

"Yeah."

"How many times did my mother call?"

"A few times."

"At least three times the first day and twice the second day." We turned up Amsterdam Avenue. The kids from J.H.S. 43 were just getting out, and I had to almost shout to get Styx to hear me.

"Well, she only called me twice the whole week I was in computer camp during the Easter break. I should have *known* something was up."

"She say anything about your father when she called?" Styx asked.

"The second time she called she said he was there. But I figured he was probably just in the country for a few days and dropped by to say hello or something. You know—grab a cup of coffee and get on back to the Middle East where he was working."

"You have to miss him," Styx says.

"All we've seen of the dude for the last eight

4

years is the monthly check that Mom gets," I said. "Last June I bought the mailman a Father's Day present."

"So what are they actually doing?"

"What they are actually doing is dating," I said. "That is what they are doing. Now ask me what *he* is doing."

"What's your father doing?" Styx jumped back on the curb as a gypsy cab cut in front of us.

"Mr. Paul Douglas is making them bad noises like he want to be somebody's daddy," I said. "You know, talking to me about life with a capital *L*, and stuff like that."

"You want to come to my house and tube out awhile?" Styx asked.

Styx has got this dynamite television set. It's about a hundred inches wide and ninety high. When you tube out with Styx, you are seriously tubed out! I wanted to, but I couldn't make it.

"I got to turn in my Study Skills notebook tomorrow," I said. "Or I won't get a grade on it, and my final grade will be 79 instead of the 82 I so richly deserve."

"Friday's the last day of school," Styx said.

"And today being Wednesday does not give The Mouse a whole lot of time to be making up a whole notebook," I said.

5

"How are you going to do it?"

"The divine Sheri Jones, having already copped an A, has consented to let me use her notebook as a model."

"And she just let you take it?" Styx said as we stopped in front of his crash. "That's not like Sheri, man."

"You just don't appreciate The Mouse's charm," I said.

"It's got to be something," Styx said. "See you tomorrow."

I watched the Styx take his front stairs two at a time, dodge around a guy playing checkers with himself, and disappear. Styx is my ace, my main man, my mighty wonder on the court, and my mighty thunder off the court. He's fourteen, the same age as The Mouse, and we are both wonders, each in our own special way. I might be just a little better-looking than he is, but I don't hold that against him. Oh yeah, and I guess I'm a lot more charming.

I am not that big a dude. Five foot three and three-quarter inches exactly. I weigh in at one hundred and twenty-seven and one-half pounds in sneakers and one hundred and twenty-seven and three-quarter pounds in shoes. So you kind of see where Mouse comes from. My real name is Fred, but only lames call me that.

6

Check out Styx. He is six foot three inches tall. Did you hear that? *Six foot three inches tall.* He's so big that when we walk down the street I got to decide if I want to walk on his sunny side and cop the vitamin D or his shady side to relax my tan. And he plays ball. Did I say he plays ball? He is righteous! The man can shoot from the outside. The man can shoot from the inside. He can slam, he can jam, he can do the Whimmy Wham! And if you don't know what that means it don't matter because whatever it means, you can't stop him from doing it. That's how good he is.

And check this out. He don't even like to play ball. No lie. He's into art. He does a little photography, a little music, a little chess. He hoops when there's nothing else to do.

Me, I can hoop. I can definitely hoop. I ain't jamming but I'm scamming. You may look great but you will look late. You got the ball against me and you blink and all you got left is the stink because I got the ball and gone. I played one on one with my shadow and my shadow couldn't keep up. But that's about all I do, which is now a problem since my dad is living in the city and dropping by all the time.

"Is that all you do?" he asked. "Play basketball?"

"I watch television," I said. I knew that wasn't

going to get it, but I couldn't think of anything that quick.

"Watching television is hardly *doing* something," he says.

About the third time he ran that down it began to wear heavy on The Mouse's ear, but then I peeped his hole card. See, I was *supposed* to feel bad. Then he was going to run his play about how we could do things together. Then Moms was supposed to check that out and get all teary-eyed so he could make his main play, which I figured had to be to get back together with Moms.

A word about Moms. She works for the telephone company. She is smart, and she is real cute in an almost foxy kind of way. She's little, too, like yours truly. But mainly she is good people. I can see why Pops wants to get back with her, but I can't see why he ever split in the first place. The way I figure, if you stay, you own the day, if you stray—stay away!

Okay. The Mouse comes up with a plan. I got to find something heavy to do over the summer so I can tell Mr. D (I'm not calling him Dad) that I'm too busy to be doing anything he wants to do. This shouldn't be that much of a problem because there's always something going on in the neighborhood.

I reached my building and started upstairs to

my crash. On the way I see Mrs. Tice. Mrs. Tice is a snap. Every day she takes her cat out for a walk. No lie. She got a little ugly cat named Blackstone and she takes him out for a walk on a leash. She's nosy, too.

"Hello, Mouse, how are you?"

"Fine, ma'am," I say.

"You know, that man I saw your mother with the other day looks just like an insurance salesman I used to know," she said. "Does he sell insurance?"

"I don't know what he does," I said. "I see him hanging around the house a lot, though."

Her mouth fell open, but before she could get herself in gear to ask the next question I was gone.

Sheri had a nice notebook, but she must have written down everything the guy said from the time he entered the classroom on the first day. I got writer's cramp just looking at it. Hey, but education is the key to success, right? So I started copying her notebook.

The phone rang and it was Styx. Jimmy Montgomery had just called and told him that something was going on in the park.

"Jimmy said there's a television truck and everything," Styx said over the phone.

I slipped on a shirt and headed toward the park.

☆

9

Everybody and their mama was in the park. It was June, and the kids were revving up for the rest of summer. I looked around until I found the guys I hung out with. Styx was already there, Jimmy was there, and Omega Taylor, and Toast. Beverly and Sheri were there, too. Styx and I climbed up on the fence so we could see over the crowd of kids. Beverly and Sheri went on down front.

We watched them as they finished setting up the television camera and then some guy came up and they started interviewing him. I didn't know who the guy was, but he looked familiar. He was too old to be a ballplayer, so I figured he might have been an announcer or something from the N.B.A. Margie Davis, the lady from Channel 5, was interviewing the guy but we couldn't hear what they were talking about.

I've been secretly in love with Margie Davis for almost two years. I watch the six-o'clock news just because of her.

Okay, they finish talking to the guy, and who do you think Margie Davis turns to? Beverly! It could have been me if I had gone down there with them.

Beverly is new to the neighborhood. She came from some place called Eureka in California. I don't know that much about her, just that she hit it off with Sheri pretty good. That and she's got these really fly eyes. In fact, she's so fly she's almost airborne. She would have been definitely star material if she hadn't been just a little too tall for me. Another thing—she knows she's fine. If she catches you dribbling your eyeballs in her court too long she gives you this big wink.

Now Sheri is one of these strange chicklets. When you first scope her you think that she's kind of fine, but not really outrageous. Then you get to know her and you find out she's one of these superserious people. Whatever she does she's got to get it right. But she's cool, too. She can get up to where she wants to be and get down when she wants to be. In other words if she catch you wrong she'll sing her song, run it by and signify Definitely drop the word on you.

Beverly and Sheri have another friend. Her name's Ceil and her mom's from Mexico. Ceil is cool, but Sheri said that her mom is having fits because Ceil isn't Mexicana enough. That's the main thing that moms are for, I think, having fits. The three of them—Beverly, Sheri, and Ceil—call themselves The Selects.

"So now that you're a star," I said to Beverly, "shine your light on us poor mortals and tell us what they were talking about."

"You remember that guy on television who

11

found that sunken treasure off Canada?" Beverly asked. It was hot and she was taking off her sweater.

"Yeah, I remember it," Omega said. "Found some gold doubloons and some silver."

"That was the guy they were interviewing," Beverly said. "He thinks there's a treasure around here."

"A ship went down in Harlem?"

"No, some big-time crook was supposed to have hid his money in a building around here," Beverly said. "Whoever finds it can keep it because he's been dead for about thirty years and nobody can prove who the money really belongs to."

"Where is it?"

"He hasn't found it yet," Beverly said.

The interview was supposed to be on the six-o'clock news and we figured we'd all check it out to see if Beverly was going to be on television.

"I'll check you guys out later," Toast said.

"Where you running off to?" Sheri said. "I didn't finish telling you about the talent contest that Mouse is entering."

The fellows turned and looked at me, and I'm standing there with my face hanging out over my chin 'cause I don't know what the chicklet is talking about.

12

"Right," Beverly said. "Sheri, are we going to let the rest of the guys help, too?"

"Help do what?" Jimmy asked.

"Whatever it is, I ain't helping," Omega said.

Omega grabbed the ball from Jimmy, dribbled toward the basket, took one big step and laid it up.

"You hear we couldn't get into the trio section of the talent contest?" Sheri asked.

"You didn't have enough talent?" Jimmy said.

"We have enough talent, Mr. Jimmy Montgomery, but so many people entered the trio division that they closed it out. The only way we can enter the contest is in the mixed group."

"You mean boys and girls?"

"I think that's the way it should be, anyway," Sheri said. "Don't you think so?"

"And Mouse is going to dance with The Selects," Beverly said.

"No, I am not," I said.

"Come on, Mouse." Sheri nudged me with her hip. "You wouldn't want me to write something bad about you in my *notebook*, would you?"

I couldn't believe it. I thought Sheri had rained her affection on The Mouse when she lent him her notebook. Now she was hanging me out to dry. Many days of sadness.

Some little kids came and asked us to move off

the edge of the basketball court because they wanted to play a game.

"I own this park," Styx said, "and you can't play on my basketball court."

"You don't own this park," the kid said, looking at me and Sheri.

Sheri took my arm and Styx's arm and pulled us off the court. "Why don't you guys come on and dance with us?" she said. "It won't hurt, will it, Mouse?"

"I know it won't hurt," Styx said. "Because we're not doing it."

"What do you say, Mouse?" Sheri asked.

"It might not be so bad," I said with a shrug, thinking about the notebook again.

Beverly called Omega over and asked him if he would dance with The Selects and he just fell on the ground laughing.

"Pitiful thing!" Beverly shook her head and the girls left the park together.

Omega and Jimmy got into a basketball game with the little kids and me and Styx watched from the sideline.

"I was thinking about your dad," Styx said. "You know, if he does make a comeback it might be cool. My father died five years ago and I still miss him. It'll be good to have him around. No lie."

"Could be," I said. I hadn't even thought about how it would look to everybody else to have my father show up all of a sudden. Or maybe I had thought about it in the back of my mind or something like that. I don't know. Styx just pulled the thing out of the air and laid it out. That's what he's like.

We watched Jimmy and Omega cheat the little kids awhile and then I was about to leave when Pooky came into the park with Hollywood.

Pooky is this big fat guy about twenty-six. He runs a barbecue joint over on Eighth Avenue. He thinks he's sharp but what he is mostly is big and fat and corny. He has a gold tooth in the front of his mouth that he can take out if he wants to. He's always coming to the park and telling everybody what a good ballplayer he *used* to be. Anything in the world you think you can do, he *used* to do it better.

Hollywood is Pooky's monkey. That's right— he carries this monkey around with him all the time.

"Hollywood wants you!" Pooky pointed at me.

"That ugly monkey doesn't want anything except a banana," I said.

"No, he wants to have a shooting contest with you," Pooky said. "Whoever makes the most baskets gets two dollars and whoever loses got to eat the banana and go cheep-cheep-cheep."

"In the first place, that monkey doesn't have two dollars," I said.

"I got the two dollars," Pooky said, pulling out some dollar bills from his pocket. "And I got the banana."

"In the second place, a monkey can't shoot a basketball," I said.

"Then you got to win the two dollars, right?" Pooky looked at me. "Or maybe you scared to go up against Hollywood?"

All the small kids had gathered around to see Hollywood.

"You don't have a basketball," I said.

Pooky called a guy over from another court and borrowed a basketball.

"Now we got us a contest here between a ballplayer and a monkey." Pooky held his hand up as if he were announcing a game. "But we don't know who the ballplayer and who the monkey. Whoever makes the least baskets in ten tries is the monkey and whoever makes the most is the ballplayer."

"And gets the two dollars," I said.

"And gets the two dollars," Pooky said. "You want to shoot first?"

"No, Hollywood can shoot first," I said. "I've never seen a monkey shoot a basketball before."

Pooky took Hollywood right next to the basket, held him up, and gave him the basketball.

"You're putting him right on top of the basket," I said.

"You can stand here too," Pooky said.

Hollywood threw the ball against the backboard. It went in. I couldn't believe a monkey could shoot a basketball.

The second shot went in, too.

And the third. I mean the monkey was right on top of the basket—how could he miss? In fact, he didn't miss.

Pooky gave him a big kiss and threw me the basketball.

I made four baskets in a row. Then I missed.

All the little kids started jumping up and down and talking about how this monkey had beaten a kid. Some even said a "big" kid. I ever tell you I hate monkeys?

2

Phoomp! Phoomp! . . . Phoomp! Phoomp!
Phoomp Phoomp Phoomp! Phoomp! Phoomp!
High waters run fast, still waters run deep
'Cause a man look old don't mean he asleep
Those old-time dudes were big and bold
And I'm glad I heard their stories told
They were sometimes right, and sometimes
   wrong
Their days were short but their stash was long
A million bucks will blow your mind
But your hand can't spend what your eyes
   can't find
Phoomp! Phoomp! . . . Phoomp! Phoomp!
Phoomp Phoomp Phoomp! Phoomp! Phoomp!

The phone rang and Moms jumped to answer it. It was Sheri, reminding me to check out the news on the tube.

"Something happen in the neighborhood?" Mom asked.

"Yeah, there was a television outfit from Channel 5 in the park today," I said. "Something about some guy looking for treasure in Harlem."

Mom lit up the magic tube and put it on Channel 5. They were talking about unemployment. I watched as Mom settled in an overstuffed chair with her legs over the side of it, her favorite way of sitting.

Yo, check this out. Mom and me are there tubing, and a knock comes on the door. I hop up and answer it and it's Mr. Douglas, as in *D-A-D*. He comes in and pops this light kiss on Mom's cheek. Mom is still scoping the tube, dig? The Mouse is in the other chair doing the same thing. So what does Mr. D say?

"Oh, watching television?"

You figure it.

"Mouse says they were interviewing someone on television in the park today about a fifty year old treasure and it might be on the news."

"Wouldn't you prefer being called Freddie?" Mr. D turns to me and asks.

"Wouldn't I rather be called *what*?"

"Freddie," Mr. D says. "After all, that *is* your name."

"That is a big negatory," I answered. "A very big negatory."

"Oh." He lifts an eyebrow. Definitely his best move.

So now the magic tube people are talking about the budget deficit and then they get on this story about people who leave their pets a lot of money and even cars. A moment later there's old Margie Davis looking right at The Mouse and saying how this guy believes there's a treasure hidden somewhere in Harlem. Then she turns to this dude we saw in the park.

"Where did all this treasure—and I believe you said it could be well over a million dollars—come from?"

The guy flashes this big Look-Ma-I-Ain't-Got-No-Cavities smile and then starts running down his story. "It was rumored by a lot of people in the know that Tiger Moran stashed away stacks and stacks of currency before his disappearance in 1930."

"Wait a minute. Is this the same Tiger Moran that was the big-time crook?" Margie glanced at the television camera.

"Yes, it is," the guy said. "But the government never proved that Moran actually stole the money. Whoever finds the treasure is going to have to pay taxes on it, but that's all."

Then Margie said that she asked a neighborhood resident what she thought about people hunting for treasure in Harlem. The neighborhood resident was Beverly.

"I don't care if he finds it or not," Beverly said.

She smiled at the camera the same way that Margie did, and she was almost as pretty.

"That's what makes poor people poor," Dad said. "They're looking to find treasures instead of working and saving every day."

I give Mom a look and she looks away. All by myself I figured this wasn't the right time to discuss our theory on how to hit the lottery.

So I go back to my room and finish fixing up my notebook. All the time I'm working on the notebook I'm thinking about that treasure. It ain't no big thing, like I'm going to go out and hunt for it or anything, which would be like World Serious mode. No, I definitely got it in Entertainment mode, where I'm spending all this heavy cash and being cool. Definitely cool.

The next day Teach checks out the notebook and marks it all up and gives me some kind of jive

C. The same notebook that got Sheri an A only gets me a C. You figure. Whoa! It also got me out of the tenth grade. I'm off to Juniorville.

Over the next few days nothing happens except for the heat. I don't mean just hot, I mean that ain't-for-real stuff that messes with your brain.

It was one of those days and I'm lying down on the floor hoping a tired breeze would walk by when Mr. D, who had been sitting in the kitchen stuffing his face with pork chops and mashed potatoes, asked me if I would like to enter a chess tournament.

"No." Simple response. Basic. Let output be negatory. Run output.

"I thought you played chess?" Mr. D says.

"You didn't ask me if I played the game," I said. "You asked me if I wanted to play in a tournament."

"It's something to do," Mr. D said. "And it might be challenging."

"You'll probably meet a lot of interesting people," Mom said.

"I'll think about it," I said.

Saturday. My man Toast came by. Toast is really Richie Kalonowski and he was in most of my classes in school. Some guys from Philadelphia are over in the Riverside Park playground and they're looking for somebody to play against.

"They want to play for pizzas and Cokes—that's three dollars a man," Toast said. "I got the guys together. We're going to wipe these guys out."

"Toast, it's so hot I'm thinking about giving my heart the rest of the day off and you talking about playing ball?"

Mom knocks on the door and sticks her head in. "Did your father tell you that chess tournament starts today?"

So we're playing ball.

Toast is about five eleven and built like a tank. He's either Polish or Russian, depending on when you ask him. That's because his mother is Polish and his father is Russian. If he's getting along with his mother best then he says he's Polish. If he gets along with his father best then he says he's Russian.

So who's Toast got rounded up? The Mouse, Jimmy Montgomery, Styx, Omega, and him. So what do we do? We show and we blow. The first game we lose by thirty points. This team is made up of guys who play the game.

The second game we do a lot better and we only lose by fifteen points. *Adios* six dollars.

23

Omega wanted to get together after the game to talk about it. It was after one when we got back to Morningside Avenue and nobody wanted to talk about why we had lost the game. It would have been different if we had won. Everybody likes to talk about how wonderful they are.

We settled down on a park bench and Omega was asking why we thought we had lost. It's hard to figure a guy like Omega. He's not too heavy in the education department. He was in the ninth grade so long they gave him his desk when he left. But when you talked about ball he got dead serious. Losing definitely hurt this boy. This is why he was insisting that we make this careful-type analysis of the games.

We had passed the parts where we didn't score many points and the part where we couldn't stop the other team and were just getting around to who was the most stupid when Sheri and Beverly came by.

"You hear they found the treasure?" Sheri asked.

"What treasure?"

"The treasure they were looking for in Harlem," Beverly said. "Remember on Channel 5?"

"Where'd they find it?" Styx asked.

"I don't know," Sheri said, "but it's going to be

24

on television at four o'clock. Why don't you guys come up and check it out."

Omega didn't want to go—he wanted to talk about the basketball game—but everybody else wanted to go just to get away from him talking about the basketball game. Finally, Omega didn't come and Toast said he had to get home, but Jimmy, Styx, and me picked up some potato chips and started off toward Sheri's house.

Sheri lives with her mom and her grandfather. Her father was killed in Lebanon.

"I know you people ain't going to start eating that junk just before dinnertime!" Sheri's mother said. She had a husky voice just like Sheri's.

"I've got gland trouble," Styx said. "If I don't eat a certain amount of junk food every day my glands don't work right and I start getting dizzy spells."

"Me, too," I said.

"Mouse, you want me to call your mama and ask her about your dizzy spells?" Mrs. Jones asked.

"No, ma'am."

Mrs. Jones started serving us all spaghetti and meatballs and French bread. Mostly when you went to Sheri's house that's what you got. We sat on the floor to eat it, and she made sure that each of us had paper napkins.

I thought it was going to be a news program, but it wasn't. It was a special.

First they had all of these black-and-white shots of the Tiger Moran gang. Then they had newspaper clippings. One of them had Al Capone at a party. There was an arrow pointing to one of the guys in the background.

> This is Tiger Moran, perhaps not the best-known hoodlum of his era but definitely one of the shrewdest. Said to have amassed a fortune equivalent to that of the notorious Al Capone, this rumrunner and bank-stickup artist suddenly disappeared from public view in August 1930. Was he the victim of a mob rub-out? Did he go to South America where he lived until 1977 in a luxurious villa, as one rumor has it? Or did he just assume a new identity and live right here in the United States?
>
> Mr. Jay Scott Spalding, historian, adventurer, and treasure-hunter *extraordinaire*, believes that Moran did meet an untimely end, probably at the hands of Big Al Capone's henchmen. What's more important to us today is that Tiger Moran's bounty, his loot, was never recovered.

Then the guy Spalding, the same guy that was on the tube before, came on and said that he had hired two crack detectives to track down Moran's last known moves.

"And as far as we know, this is where he spent most of his time before taking that last, and fatal, ride."

The television camera moved back and you could see that Moran was standing in front of a building.

"That's that building near the elevated lines on Broadway," Beverly said.

You could see the el train and a lot of people standing on the sidewalk watching the television camera people. It was getting dark outside and beginning to rain. Some of the people had umbrellas.

"I bought this building two months ago," Mr. Spalding said. "I'll probably turn it into a crime museum."

"Using Tiger Moran's own money to do it," the announcer said.

"I sure hope so," Mr. Spalding said as he went through the open doors.

The next shot was of the inside of the building, which looked like a warehouse.

When they were ready to open the safe, the two experts moved away and Mr. Spalding tugged at it. Nothing happened. One of the experts gave him a crowbar and he put it in the crack of the door and pushed. The door came open.

You could hear somebody calling, "Get a light on the safe! Get a light on the safe!"

The light moved and then was on the safe. It was empty.

The Spalding dude looked like something thrown away. I thought the guy was going to boohoo right there on the tube. Styx asked could he switch the channel so we could watch the end of the Mets game. He switched and checked out the Mets. They were losing.

"Who they talking about there, girl?" Sheri's grandfather, we called him Gramps, stood in the doorway. He stood up straight, almost stiffly, like an old soldier.

"The Mets are playing the Expos," Sheri said.

"No, I mean before," Gramps said.

"The Tiger Moran gang," Sheri said. "They found his old headquarters and they thought he had money hidden there."

"That building they showed was over there near the train," Gramps said. "That's where the Siegel brothers used to have their headquarters. Tiger Moran wasn't nothing when he was with them. He didn't make no name for himself until he broke off with them and got his own gang."

28

"How you know so much about gangs, Daddy?" Mrs. Jones asked her father.

"They used to have their gang business," Gramps said, fishing through his pockets until he had found his pipe, "which was mostly running alcohol and the rackets and stuff like that, and then they had their regular businesses. There was two moving businesses that used to hire colored fellows a lot. Dutch Schultz had a moving and cleaning business. They used to clean offices, or maybe he'd have you clean out his club. If you wanted to work with him you lined up on 135th Street and Fifth Avenue. If they needed anybody that's where they would pick you up.

"Tiger Moran, he had him a little moving business and his drivers would pick up men on 116th Street and St. Nicholas Avenue. That's who I worked for, Tiger Moran."

"You actually worked for a hoodlum?" Styx asked.

"I didn't do no hoodlum work." Gramps shot Styx a dirty look. "They didn't allow no colored in their gangs back in them days. Not that I would have been in it if they let me."

"But you actually knew Tiger Moran?" Sheri asked.

"Didn't know him more than to pass a few

29

words with him," Gramps said. "He wasn't the kind of guy you sit and chew the fat with. When he broke off with the Siegel brothers it was me and a young boy named Herbert that moved him into his new place. A warehouse."

"You telling me that you might know where his treasure is?" Beverly asked.

I put down my spaghetti and turned to see what Gramps was going to say.

"I don't know what kind of treasure he had or he didn't have," Gramps said. "I told you I wasn't in his gang or nothing."

The score of the Mets game was two to nothing and the bases were loaded with a pinch hitter up. He hit the first pitch to left field to tie the game up. Everybody started talking about the game, but I kept thinking about Gramps and Tiger Moran.

3

Ta-Chhh Ta-Chhh! Ta-Chhh Ta-Chhh!
Ta-Chhh Ta-Chhh! Ta-Chhh Ta-Chhh!
What's cool for me ain't cool for you
But we all got to do what we all got to do
I got that rhythm, I can really work
I can pop I can break I can slide and jerk
I can party hearty, I'm the get-down king
If the deal is fresh I'll do my thing
I ain't no freak though I am unique
When I'm on the stage I just got to speak
Ta-Chhh Ta-Chhh! Ta-Chhh Ta-Chhh!
Ta-Chhh Ta-Chhh! Ta-Chhh Ta-Chhh!

☆

U.S.A. Today runs this story about how this guy
Ahmed Wilson got to go to college on a basketball

31

scholarship. You know, the whole Ghetto-to-Glory trip. Then the paper says it's going to cover his trip back to the park where he used to play ball, which of course is Morningside Park. Ahmed runs this rap about checking out how the young brothers are playing ball.

So Styx gives me a buzz and says we ought to drop by the park just to see if anybody shows. The Mouse figures that's cool so I grab my wristbands and make it on over to the playground.

When we first make the scene there aren't too many people around, but more and more people 'start to show. They're all talking about the story in the paper. Meanwhile, on the courts, the games are getting heavy. Me, Styx, and Omega get in one of those games where people just start beating on each other, the kind where you got to show blood to get a foul call. Then I look over to the side and there's my moms. That's not too bad because she likes coming to watch me play. She doesn't know much about sports but she always roots for me. In fact, she roots for everybody that plays, even if they're playing against me. But she brings Mr. D along, and he comes over and shakes my hand and wishes me luck like I'm playing for Notre Dame or somebody.

"Just remember, son, winning isn't everything.

As long as you do your best you can consider yourself a winner. In here."

The guy actually taps my chest! I look at Mom and I think she's trying not to laugh.

So I'm playing and I'm playing serious. We are definitely whipping some butt, and the little crowd that came to the park to see if the newspaper shows is all gathered around our court. This sets Omega off. I mean the dude goes *off.* The sweat's popping off my man and he's grunting and carrying on and hacking dudes to death.

We knock off about three lame squads and then this heavy squad shows up. They got this big dude everybody calls Hill 'cause that's how he big he is. They also had this other dude on their team named Bobby Burdette, who made the high school All-City team.

Omega calls us over to the side before the game and starts in with what he thinks is a pep talk. I'm retying my sneakers when I spot Beverly, Sheri, and Ceil Bonilla standing on the sideline.

The Selects started cheering for us. That made us feel good and made the other team work even harder. The game went back and forth and I figured we were in big trouble. The score was tied when I tried a hook shot from the foul line and Bobby grabbed it. That's right, folks, he didn't block it, he jumped up and grabbed the sucker.

They got up by two but Omega stole a pass and Styx jammed twice in a row to put us up by two. One more basket and we had the game.

Styx went to the corner and Omega faked a pass to him and drove for the hoop. Hill slapped it away and it came out to me. Bobby came out after me, and him and the ball arrived at almost the same time.

"Give it up, fool!"

I went up looking for somebody to pass off to. Nobody was open, and I could feel Bobby's breath in my face. I knew I couldn't come down with the ball so I flung it toward the basket.

When it swished through the net the whole park went wild.

"In your face, Bobby!" a dude called out from the sidelines.

Everybody's slapping me five as I Reebok off the court and Bobby's running after me and he's so mad he's spitting.

"You got lucky!" he says. "You got lucky! You couldn't even see the basket!"

"I was just lucky I didn't have nobody on me but you," I said.

They wanted a return match, but Omega had to split and I didn't want to play anyway.

"Where the cheerleaders?" Omega looked around for The Selects.

"They're over there talking to Mouse's folks," Styx says.

"You know why they rapping with your mama?" Omega says. " 'Cause they still trying to get us to dance with them and they got you down as the weak link."

Mom comes over and says that Sheri's mother has invited us to lunch.

"They're trying to get us to dance with them," I said.

"I know they are," Mom says.

"They've got to be kidding," Mr. D said, laughing. "I can just see you guys hopping around in tights."

I laughed, but I didn't really dig the way he said it. He didn't even know The Selects.

"Are you headed toward the house?" Mom asked.

"No, I think I'll see what Styx is doing," I said.

What Styx was doing was going to Sheri's house for lunch. Omega wasn't going, but I decided to go along.

"What do you think their plot is?" Styx asked me on the way over to Sheri's crash.

"I don't think they have a plot," I said. "I just think they find me irresistible."

☆

"What have you people been doing?" Mrs. Jones looked us over. "You boys look like you've been swimming with your clothes on. And you don't smell too good, either."

"Where's Gramps?" Sheri asked.

"He's in the living room watching his cartoons," Mrs. Jones said. Then she went and got two washcloths. She gave me one and the other one she gave to Styx and pointed toward the bathroom.

"You don't have to get all the stink off," she said. "Just get enough off so's you don't be killing my houseplants."

Embarrass. Anyway, Styx and I go into the bathroom and start washing up. We're still trying to figure out what's up with The Selects.

"Maybe they're going to be real nice and hope it rubs off on us," Styx said.

"They're scheming and dreaming, but it's got to be more than that," I said. "Sheri and Beverly are definitely Gucci-Poochies, but Ceil's over here, too. I think they're going to make some kind of move."

"It won't work," Styx said, putting out his hand.

"No lie!" I gave him five.

By the time Styx and I got out, the girls had settled in the living room with Gramps. Just from the way they were looking I could tell something was up. Mrs. Jones was there, too.

"So tell us more about the Tiger Moran gang, Gramps," Sheri said, looking over at me and Styx.

Now, The Mouse is waiting for the fast pitch about dancing with The Selects and Sheri is backing up and throwing a curve about Tiger Moran. I look over toward Styx and he looks back at me and shrugs.

"Ain't what you call no whole lot to tell," Gramps said. "Like I told you before, there used to be a lot of gangs in Harlem in them days. There was your colored gangs, and there was your Italian gangs over on the East Side, and there was a German gang that used to come around ever so often. Each gang had its own little thing."

"What was Tiger Moran's gang," Mrs. Jones asked, "Irish?"

"You want to tell this story?" Gramps gave his daughter a mean look, and she shut up.

I made a mental note about how that mean look looked so I could use it later.

"Tiger Moran used to be with the German gang for a while and then he set out on his own," Gramps went on. "He didn't have no special kind

37

of people in his gang, either. Except they were all white, of course. You didn't have a lot of mingling in them days. Anyway, Tiger went around and got whoever he wanted in his gang. You had to be smart because he wasn't into no head knocking and shooting people up. He had what you would call a modern gang.

"Like I said, I used to work for him now and then." Gramps had one of those pipes that was covered with leather. He took it out and put it in his mouth. He didn't light it up or anything, just put it in one side of his mouth. "Tiger owned two warehouses that I know of, and he owned a bar over past Fifth Avenue where the White Rose used to be before the city closed it down."

"Tell us where you think he stashed the money," Sheri said.

Sheri's got this big smile on her face and I know something's up. So I just settle down and put the brain on Super Scope and kick in about another meg of random access memory.

"He could have burned it up for all I know," Gramps said.

"You really think he burned it?" Styx asked. He had two hands full of potato chips.

"He might have," Gramps said. "Or he could have stashed it. He had a secret hideout over near the Sinclair Ink Company. I knew it was somewhere over there, but I never did know exactly where. In them days you didn't want to go around nosing where you didn't belong. One time I was working on one of his moving trucks—mostly we moved stuff for whoever Tiger's customers was— but this one time two of Tiger's boys picked us up and took us over to the warehouse. They said that Tiger wanted some of his own personal stuff moved. We loaded a piano and some trunks onto the back of a truck.

"That piano was pretty heavy but the trunks didn't have no real heavy weight to them," Gramps said. "But they felt like two tons when we tried to lift them onto the back of the truck."

"If they weren't heavy, how could they feel like two tons?" I asked.

"What's your name, boy?"

"Mouse."

"Mouse?" Gramps took his pipe out of the side of his mouth and leaned toward me. "What kind of a tomfool name is that?"

"That's just what they call me," I said. "My real name is Frederick."

"That ain't much better," Gramps said. "Anyway, you ever try lifting anything with a fellow holding a machine gun staring down your eyeballs?" Gramps asked.

"No, sir."

"That's how we had to load them trunks. I prayed to God that I didn't have to sneeze or nothing. Whatever was in them trunks had to be something pretty important.

"Me and Herbie had to sit in the back of the truck and one of Tiger's boys—they called him Sudden Sam—sat back there with us holding the machine gun.

"After a while the truck stopped and Tiger Moran himself got in. He was all dappered out in a pinstripe suit and tie and had him a flower in his lapel.

" 'Pay these boys and let them go,' he said. 'We'll finish the job ourselves.'

"So we got paid off and got out the truck right down from the police station on LaSalle Street," Gramps said. "That was about two, maybe three days after the Fourth. If Tiger Moran was really stashing a lot of money, that was it."

"And you think he took it to the gang's headquarters?" Mrs. Jones asked.

"I guess he did something with it," Gramps said. "I know he wasn't letting me and Herbie know where he was taking it."

"Everybody in his gang is probably dead by now," Styx said.

"Everybody except Sudden Sam," Gramps said. "He ain't dead."

Shhh Shhh Shhh! Sh! Sh!
Shhh Shhh Shhh! Sh! Sh!
You got to be strong when the deal go down
Or you'll hear the squeal all over town
And when you get them chumped-off blues
You look for a way to pay your dues
But best remember what saves your skin
Can be the same little number that does you in
Like the puppet man, just doing his thing
You just don't know who pulling your string
Shhh Shhh Shhh! Sh! Sh!
Shhh Shhh Shhh! Sh! Sh!

"Who's Sudden Sam?" Styx asked.

Before Gramps could answer, Sheri got up and

41

said she smelled the soup.

Sheri's mother told us to come into the kitchen for dinner and we did. She served the soup and I could already smell the sauce for the tacos. Mrs. Jones could cook. I mean she could *burn*. Me and Styx alone ate enough tacos to reduce the taco population of the world by half. Beverly, Ceil, and Sheri didn't do so bad, either. Gramps stayed in the living room, and when we were done eating I was ready to go back and finish the conversation with him.

"Anybody know what time it is?" Sheri asked as I wiped my face with a napkin.

"It's five thirty," Ceil said.

"Oh, then I've got to study," Sheri said, getting up from where she had been sitting cross-legged on the floor. "I want to keep up my schoolwork over the summer. Maybe we can get together tomorrow or later in the week and work on our dancing, okay?"

I glanced over at Styx and started to smile as Sheri took me by the elbow. In another minute me, Styx, Beverly, and Ceil were out in the hallway. Styx still had his napkin in his hand.

"Yo, man, what am I doing in the hallway?" I asked.

"What are we all doing in the hallway?" Styx added.

"Sheri had to study," Beverly said.

"Unh-uh." Styx shook his head. "We just got put out."

"I think she really wants to study," Ceil chimed in. "She was talking about it before."

I looked at Styx and Styx looked at me. The girls were making their move but I still didn't dig what it was.

"I was just getting into the story about the gang," Styx said. "You know, I was thinking—"

"It was probably rough to be in one of those old-time gangs," Ceil interrupted.

Okay, so The Mouse is cool. Me and Styx had just been hustled into a quick good-bye from Sheri's crash and now we're supposed to ask a whole lot of questions about what's happening. No way. If you're going to play a game then call my name 'cause I can game with the best.

"So you think it was rough in the olden days?" I said as we went outside.

"Sure, you could get rubbed out anytime," Ceil went on. "One minute you could be walking up the street, and the next minute one of those old-time black limousines comes down the street and bang! You're a headline."

"If you know you might get crapped out any minute you got to keep your crap rap handy," I said. "Just in case."

"That's just in the movies," Beverly said. "In real life you don't have a chance to make a dying speech."

"I'd be ready," I said.

"Let's check it out," Beverly said. "You're walking down the street and I'm in the car getting ready to shoot you, okay?"

"Yeah, come on."

We walked down past some girls jumping double Dutch on the sidewalk.

"You lean against that wall," Beverly said, pointing to the wall next to the community center.

I did it and Beverly started slowly down the sidewalk making believe she was steering a car. When she got near me I dove to the sidewalk.

"Hey, you don't know I'm out to get you," Beverly said. "I'm an out-of-town hood. You don't even recognize me."

"Okay." I got up and walked a little farther. Styx is checking this all out and wondering where it's going. I slip him a wink and keep on with the game.

Beverly was coming from the back.

"What you smiling about, buddy?" She made believe she was leaning out the window of the car.

"Just having a nice day," I called back.

Then she drove past me and I asked her how come she didn't shoot and she said she was just checking out my habits so she was sure not to miss me.

"Beverly sounds like a real hit woman," Styx said.

He was smiling. I wasn't smiling because I didn't like the whole thing anymore. I knew it was a game and everything, but I didn't like the idea of Beverly just riding around getting ready to take a shot at me, even if it was imaginary. She seemed to be enjoying it too much.

She came around again, smiled, then pointed her finger at me. "Bang!"

I staggered around a little, just to make it look good, then closed my eyes and fell to the ground.

"Oh no, he's been shot!" Ceil said. Then she got down on one knee. "Wait a minute. He's saying something."

"I lived a good life," I said. "But now my time has come. I want everybody to remember me the way I used to be, a carefree playboy."

"Hah!" Beverly's two cents.

"I have lived a good life," I went on. "But now I must go to that great gangland in the sky."

"If you killed anybody or robbed a bank or

45

something, you could go to the other place," Ceil said.

"It's right that I'm laying here dying on the street," I said, ignoring her. "Because these streets have been my home ever since I ran away from the orphanage. I knew I had to run away to get food for my little brother, who wasn't being fed except once a day."

"Hey, you got a cool dying speech," Beverly leaned over and looked down at me. "Go on, man."

"I couldn't find a job so I had to steal from grocery stores, and then I began stealing from banks—"

"What he doing down there?" Mrs. Roosevelt, a short, fat woman with glasses that sat on the end of her nose, looked down at me.

"He's giving his dying speech," Styx said.

"He don't look like he dying none to me," she said in this real flat voice.

"He just pretending to be dying." Ceil shaded her eyes with her hand. "He wants to practice his dying speech."

"That's the dumbest thing I ever seen in my life," Mrs. Roosevelt said. "Your mama know you laying out in the street getting your clothes filthy?"

"Maybe you'd better get up," Beverly said.

"No, he don't have to get up." Mrs. Roosevelt was going through her pocketbook. She found what she was looking for. "Here, stick him with this pin so he can pretend he dying in pain."

"Yo, lady. You getting carried away," I said.

She let out this real high laugh and went on down the street shaking her head.

Did I tell you I hate it when old ladies crack on me?

When we split from Bev and Ceil, Styx asked me what was going on. I'm not sure if the boy is slow or if he just appears slow when he's around The Mouse.

"What did you hear at Sheri's crash?" I asked.

"Just her grandfather talking about the gang," Styx said.

"That's got to be the key," I said. "Let's go to the videotape. Replay the scene and what do you get?"

"Soups and tacos," Styx said. "And Gramps."

"And some talk about Tiger Moran's hideout," I said. "Now what we're supposed to do is to get all excited about maybe finding the hideout or something and then we volunteer to dance with The Selects. Dig?"

"And they think that lame action is going to

47

work?" Styx asked.

"With weaker minds it probably would," I said.

☆

Okay, so it's Tuesday and it looks like it's going to rain but it don't. The Mouse, ever cool, turns on the sound box to check out the weather. Everything is supposed to clear up. The mother person knocks on the door, sticks her head in, and announces that she's ready to leave for work.

"There are eggs in the refrigerator," she says.

"That's a good place to keep the eggs," I say.

The mother person takes a softball from The Mouse's dresser and throws it at The Mouse, right? No, she fakes the throw, then throws it *after* The Mouse has made his move and hits The Mouse. Either the mother person is getting slick or The Mouse needs some new moves.

"And there's ice cream in the freezer," the mother person adds. She throws The Mouse a kiss and splits.

I call my man Styx and he tells me he has to go to the dentist.

"Just keep your mouth shut and everything will be cool," I say.

I call my man Omega and his mom says he has to work with his father. His father owns a refrigerator repair business and he wants Omega to get

48

into it. Omega wants to go to play ball but his father don't dig no ball.

The next ringy-dingy is to my man Toast. My man Toast says he's glad I called because he was just going swimming with some other dudes and I could go with him. I said I had an ear infection and couldn't go in the water. Toast did not have to know that The Mouse was not too cool beneath the H_2O.

The Mouse decided to go to the park by himself.

There were a million kids in the park. Ceil's mom works in the park teaching the kids folk dancing and stuff like that, and so the girls were there helping her out. When they see me they come over and start talking about how cool it was that Gramps knew all about Tiger Moran and everything.

"Why don't you get the guys to come up to my house this evening," Sheri said. "Maybe he'll tell us some more about the gangsters."

"And maybe while we're there we can practice dancing or something, huh?" I said.

"Mouse, don't be jive," Sheri said.

She went on back to helping with the folk dancing and I watched some little kids playing ball. Beverly and Ceil were sitting on the bench with me and I was waiting for them to start in on the dancing again when who comes into the park but Bobby Burdette and his crew.

Now Bobby Burdette, beside being a not-too-bad ballplayer, is a Class A jerk. I think the fool has chronic distemper. He shows up with some of his friends, all as ugly as he is, and gives me this warm greeting:

"Hi, punk!"

"Yo, man. The name is not punk," I said.

"When I call out the word 'punk' you'd just better answer." Bobby sat on the back of the bench with his feet on the seat.

"You better be careful, Bobby," Leroy, one of his friends, said. "Mouse is liable to go upside your head."

"Go upside my head?" Bobby looked at me and spit on the ground. "He'd rather take a sandwich out a mountain lion's mouth than mess with me."

"I don't know, he looking at you kind of hard," Leroy said. "He got his ladies here checking him out, too. He liable to do anything."

"He can look but he'd better not leap," Bobby said. " 'Cause if he do I'm gonna sow what his jaw can't reap."

"How come you guys can't get along?" Ceil asked.

"Bobby is mad because we beat him playing ball the other day," I said.

"You got lucky," Bobby said. "You couldn't even see the basket when you shot."

"I saw it good enough to burn you," I said, my mouth slipping into gear.

"Only reason he talking that trash is 'cause he know the park man won't let me knock him out in here," Bobby said.

"Why don't you fight at five thirty?" These words fell upon my ears directly from the mouth of Beverly.

"That's okay with me," Bobby said, as I turned to look at Beverly.

"The park man leaves at five," she went on. "We can all come back here and—Wait, I got to go shopping with my mother this afternoon. Can we make it tomorrow at five thirty? Okay?"

"Yeah, that's cool with me," Bobby said.

Now The Mouse is standing there in Numb City while this chicklet is steady sliding syllables between his body and Good Health.

Bobby's friends started talking about how I was too scared to show up and then Beverly started talking about how I wasn't scared. I was waiting for the commercial because this had to be some kind of cartoon or something.

51

"You have to answer right now," Beverly said, turning to me. "Are you going to show up to fight or are you just a pink-toed, yellow-livered, nose-picking mamma's boy?"

Good question.

"Yeah, I'll be here," I said. My stomach heard what my mouth was saying and was trying to crawl up my windpipe to shut it up.

Everybody was saying stuff like *Ooooh!* and *Aaaaah!* and how they didn't know I had so much heart. If they had come a little closer they could have heard the sucker beating.

I was scared and Bobby was mad. He started punching his fist into his hand and giving me mean looks. He'd punch his fist into his hand and then he'd give it a couple of twists, just to dig the pain in. He was hitting himself hard enough to break his fingers. What would he do to me?

Now, the real bad thing about this whole scene was that I had to hang around. I just couldn't go home and get in the closet and cry like I wanted to. The Mouse is a lover and a ballplayer—he is not a fighter. Now I had to sit there while old dumb-butt Leroy talked about how I was going to mess Bobby up. And old dumb Bobby sat there listening to dumb-butt Leroy and got madder and madder.

It took one minute and seven seconds before the word got all over the playground. People I didn't even know came over to offer me little bits of encouragement.

"Hey, Mouse, you gonna get killed!"

"You better put a name tag on your big toe so your family know who you are when the fight's over!"

"Can we go to your house for pizza after your funeral?"

Friendly little stuff like that. I just smiled and shook my head like I wasn't scared or anything. It was almost funny, but then Bobby ruined it.

The playground had this heavy punching bag that hung from a platform. Somebody dragged it out and put a sign on it that said MOUSE. Bobby took off his shirt and started punching the bag.

Whomp! Whomp! Whomp!

That's all you could hear in the playground.

Whomp! Whomp! Whomp!

Some little kids on a field trip stood around and watched. They were impressed. Leroy called me over to watch and I walked over and sort of laid my head to one side and watched Bobby hit that bag.

When I got closer I noticed that the *Whomp! Whomp! Whomp!* wasn't the only thing you could

53

hear when you were close. You could also hear Bobby grunting as he threw a punch. It sounded more like this:

Grunt-*WHOMP!*   Grunt-*WHOMP!*   Grunt-*WHOMP!*

I figured all that grunting probably meant that he wasn't in too good a shape because the harder he hit the bag the harder he grunted. He was sweating a lot, too. The sweat ran down from the muscles on his arms, which were about as big as my legs, to the muscles on his legs, which were about as big as my waist. I knew with all that grunting and sweating he could only whomp me fifty or sixty times before he got tired.

"Hey, Mouse, eat some of this chicken so you can build your strength up." Fatty Thompson came up to me with a half a hamburger in his hand.

"Go finish your hamburger," I said.

"This ain't no hamburger," he said, looking at me like I was crazy. "This is fried chicken."

"I know a hamburger when I see it," I said.

"Huh?" Fatty looked at his burger. "Oh, I see what you mean. This *was* some fried chicken before Bobby hit it and turned it into hamburger!"

Then he laughed his high laugh and slapped his fat leg.

☆

"You got to be kidding!" This is what Styx said when I called him later to tell him what happened in the park.

"If I was kidding why am I calling up all my friends to tell them good-bye?" I said, shifting the phone to my other shoulder.

"What did you say to Beverly?"

"Nothing. She just walked away like it was no big deal," I said. "I went up to her, but I was so mad I was thinking in rectangles and talking in Dog."

"You're not going to fight Bobby, are you?" Styx asked.

"I think I got to, man," I said.

"Why?"

"Everyone's going to say I'm a punk if I don't," I said.

"Hey, I won't think you're a punk if you don't go getting beat up because of some girl's big mouth," Styx said. "Think about it."

When I hung up I switched the Brain Box to Truly Deep and did some heavy grinding. Styx was right. I didn't really have to get beaten up for nothing. And it was really cool of him to say that he didn't think I was a punk if I didn't fight Bobby. But check it out—everybody was waiting for The Mouse to punk out. If I didn't show, it would be like they had all peeped my hole card.

I didn't know what to do. I wanted to call Styx again to see if he could convince me not to get myself humangilated.

I skipped supper. I didn't want to eat. I didn't want to do anything. I didn't even put the tube on. I just stared at the ceiling. It was a nice ceiling and I had spent a lot of my life staring at it. I realized I wouldn't live to benefit from all the study assignments and homework I had been given through the years and that I had been right not to have done most of them.

"Are you all right?" The mother person peeked in.

"Yeah," I said.

"I'm not so sure." Mom came in and put her hand on my forehead to see if I had a fever.

"Do I have a fever?" I said a quick prayer. If I had a fever they'd have to cancel the fight. Wouldn't they?

"No, you feel fine," Mom said.

"Thanks, Mom."

"Get some rest," she said.

I thought about Beverly. I hadn't known her

that long. She had moved to our neighborhood from California and had hit it off with Sheri pretty good. Maybe she had left a whole chain of broken bodies behind her in California. No wonder she was so interested in my dying speech.

5

Ka-phoomp! Ka-phoomp! Da Doom Da Dooom!
Ka-phoomp! Ka-phoomp! Da Doom Da Dooom!
Your eyes may shine and your sweat may pop
But there ain't no win for you to cop
'Cause a Kung Fu mama don't play around
Bip! Bip! Bip! You're on the ground
Your head goes funny and your legs go weak
And your raps sound just like pigeon Greek
You slide away like old King Tut
'Cause Kung Fu Mama has whipped your butt
Ka-phoomp! Ka-phoomp! Da Doom Da Dooom!
Ka-phoomp! Ka-phoomp! Da Doom Da Dooom!

What the world had to understand is that The
Mouse was definitely made for the better things

58

in life. The better things in life being good food, cable on the tube, and maybe a motorized skateboard. The motorized skateboard didn't have to come right away. I wasn't in a hurry. Good things did not include a fight with Bobby Burdette.

I closed my eyes and scoped the future. There I was, lying on the ground, a beaten, bloody mess. Little kids were standing around and shaking their heads. Bobby Burdette was looking down on me and feeling sorry for what he had done. A dark cloud passed overhead. The future was bleak.

A knock came on the door. I thought it was fate but it was only Mom again. "There's a young lady here to see you."

I didn't feel like seeing any young lady. Especially a young lady named Beverly.

"Hi. I'm going for a walk," she said. "You want to come along?"

"No way."

"You're not upset about Bobby?"

"I am very upset about Bobby," I said.

"I'm really sorry," she said in this real sweet voice. "Can we take a walk and talk about it? Please?"

"Yeah. Okay."

I told Mom I'd be back in an hour or so and she said she'd keep my dinner warm. "Are you sure you feel well enough to go for a walk?" she asked.

"I guess so." The Mouse nodded glumly.

"It's a nice evening," Beverly's saying as we start down the stairs.

"If you say so," I said. "The Selects were dancing tonight?" She was wearing those little slipper-type shoes.

"Unh-uh," she said. She gave me this funny little smile. I remembered a story we read in school once about these weird chicklets in ancient Greece and how they would sing and lure sailors to their deaths.

We get downstairs and who's there but Ceil and Sheri. They're smiling, too. It's like a whole smile festival except for me—I'm still fighting back the tears. Before I know it they're walking me down the street and talking about how nice the weather has been.

"What's up?" I asked.

"We're just out taking a walk," Ceil said. "You don't like walks?"

Okay, I've got butterflies in my stomach and they're trying to get out in the worst way and these three chicklets are walking me around the neighborhood. I figure Beverly is sorry for what she's done and they're trying to figure a way to save me. We walked down to 119th Street past a steel-drum band and a guy dressed like an Arab

60

selling incense and oils. Sheri let the guy put some oil on her wrist, sniffed at it, and said she might buy some the next time she saw him.

"Oh, let's go in here," Beverly said.

I looked up to see where "here" was. It was the Clarion, a rundown apartment building.

"What's in here?" I asked.

"Oh, you'll see," Beverly said. "C'mon."

"Yo, squeal the deal." The Mouse stopped in his tracks. "What is going down?"

"It's a shortcut," Beverly says.

Sheri's giggling. It's execution eve and they're running games.

"Beverly, do you *know* where we're going?" I asked as she took my hand and started into the backyard past a row of trash cans.

"I think so," she said.

When I saw what was in the backyard I didn't believe it. That is, my eyes believed it but the rest of me didn't. It was Bobby Burdette! He was leaning against the fence smoking a cigarette. At first he don't scope us cause he got his earphones stuck into his headbone and he's steady pumping boom box. Then he scopes the dopes, debones the phones, and stands up.

"What you doing here, punk?" He glared at me.

Another good question. My whole body fell

61

apart. My legs started to run but my feet didn't move, which explained why my knees looked like they were shaking.

"I don't think you should call Mouse a punk," Beverly said. "I think you should take that back."

"I'm gonna take it back, all right," Bobby said, his nostrils snorting two kinds of pollution. "I'm gonna knock his punk head off!"

He almost got to where I was standing before I could blink an eye. I said almost because he didn't quite make it. Beverly screamed and went flying through the air. My heart most stopped cold.

She landed that slipper she was wearing right in the middle of Bobby's chest. He flew backward and landed on his back. He didn't know what to do and neither did I. He looked down at his chest and up at Beverly, who was standing there with one arm out and the other one at her side in a Kung Fu stance. I looked back at Bobby as he made a face and got slowly up on his feet. I really wasn't that worried because I knew my moms had Blue Cross.

Pip! Pip!

It sounded like the snapping of a towel. It was just that quick, too. Beverly jumped in front of Bobby and hit him twice in the stomach. He doubled over. Then she went into a spin and hit him with a side kick behind the legs. He went up in the air and landed hard on his back. Beverly looked like she was really digging the set.

Meanwhile Sheri and Ceil are leaning against the building watching the whole thing like it's showtime at the Apollo and Beverly's on.

Bobby got to his feet again. He took a half step toward Beverly. He didn't know if he should look at her feet or at her hands. She lifted her hands toward him and then kicked him on the side of his head.

"I really don't want to hurt you a lot," she said, looking down at him and talking into the ear he wasn't holding. "So you want to give it up now?"

He nodded.

"I think you should say you're sorry to Mouse," Ceil said.

Bobby looked at me. "Yeah, yeah."

"If I see you in the playground tomorrow at five thirty, I'll know you want to finish this," Beverly said. "And I won't be so easy on you the next time. You dig?"

We left Bobby sitting there. I think he was still stunned. So was I.

"So what do you think, Mouse?" Beverly asks me when we get back in the street.

"Are you a . . . ? I mean . . . that was pretty cool."

"I just can't stand bullies," she said.

"Hey, I just got an idea!" Sheri said. "Since you're not going to be fighting Bobby tomorrow, why don't you come over and practice with us?"

"Well . . . I . . ." I was stammering again. Stammering and wondering how I was going to explain to Styx and everybody that I was going to be dancing with The Selects. Hey, it was easier than explaining how I got my body rearranged, so I said I would definitely be there.

"And what about Styx?"

"Styx?"

"Since Beverly did save your life," Sheri said, smiling sweetly, "perhaps you could put in a word to your friend Styx about how you would like him to dance with us, too."

"Since Beverly saved my . . . ?"

The Mouse had been had. His body had been thrown into the arena with the lions just to get him to dance with The Selects. Not only that but part of the price was to get Styx to dance, too. Life did have its little problems.

I got home and the moms person noticed that I was looking better.

64

"That young lady wasn't your girlfriend, was she?" Mom asked.

"Not really," I said. "Just somebody I get a kick out of."

Ooch Ch-Bow Bow Bow! Ooch Ch-Bow!
Ooch Ch-Bow Bow Bow! Ooch Ch-Bow!
Now Sudden Sam is a mighty dude
His voice is rough and his walk is crude
He was the mighty big bosser and heavy
   enforcer
The main out-tosser and the pain endorser
He ran with a crew and you got to know
They were def with the games of long ago
Tiger Moran was the man with the flash
And he really knew how to stash the cash
Ooch Ch-Bow Bow Bow! Ooch Ch-Bow!
Ooch Ch-Bow Bow Bow! Ooch Ch-Bow!

"Har-har!" Styx laughed over the phone. "You hear what happened to Omega?"

"Har-har? What kind of phony laugh is that?" The Mouse asks.

"It's not a phony laugh," Styx said. "I just think it was funny what happened to him."

"What happened?"

"Sheri found out that he wouldn't be eligible to play ball next season unless he passes a math test at the start of the term."

"You think that's funny?"

"Well, not really." Styx kind of drawled the words out. "But Sheri said that she would coach him if he danced with The Selects."

"I bet he cracked up when he heard that."

"No, he didn't," Styx said. "He's going to dance with them."

"Omega's going to dance? In public? In the park?" I fell back on the bed. Another guy had bit the dust. "Yeah, and I heard you were dancing, too," Styx said.

"Heh, heh, heh."

"What kind of a phony laugh is that?" Styx asked.

"Look, I'm only dancing because the chicklets really need me," I said. "You know, equal opportunity and all that."

"Well, they're not getting me to dance, that's for sure," Styx said.

"So you're not interested in the . . . in the hunt for Tiger Moran's stash?" I asked, revving up my brain.

"What does that have to do with anything?" Styx asked.

"Look, Styx." I shifted my position on the bed. "I didn't want to say this to you, but the *real* reason I'm dancing is to get close to the girls when they start looking for the treasure. I mean, the moment I heard that Gramps knew Tiger Moran . . ."

"Mouse, you are lying through your Mousey teeth," Styx said. "The last time we talked you were ready to put a serious hurting on Beverly. Now you want to dance with her. What gives?"

"So maybe I thought Beverly wasn't too cool, but I guess she's okay," I said. "Actually, she got me out of the fight with Bobby."

"How did she do that?"

"She kind of beat him up, man!"

"Did you say she ate him up?"

"No, she *beat* him up," I said again. "She's into Kung Fu."

"So she set up the fight just to have an excuse to beat up Bobby?"

68

"I guess," I said.

"Or does she like you?"

"Possible," I said. "Possible. But what I would really dig is if you would give them a hand, too. If we copped a prize it would be cool. And I can't figure us doing anything and not winning the sucker. Not only that but it's something to do."

"I'll think about it," Styx said.

I thought that Styx would go along with the program. He was the kind of guy who was always interested in doing something new. Dancing would be new and so would looking for Tiger Moran's old hideout if we got around to that. It looked like the summer was shaping up.

The more I thought about things the more I dug it. Actually it might have been my near brush with death at the hands of Bobby Burdette that gave me a new outlook on life. Everything seemed wonderful. By the time Mr. D came around I didn't even mind seeing him. I told him about the dancing and was about to tell him about Tiger Moran when I dug that his jaws were tight over something. What it turned out to be was that he and Mom had had an argument.

Mr. D asked me if I thought he should get her some flowers. I shrugged it off. I mean you can't be telling no dude how to get over with your mama, even if he is your dad.

☆

Wednesday morning. Sheri called and asked if Styx was going to dance. I told her he told me he would think about it. I was going to tell her that he was interested in finding out more about Tiger Moran but she beat me to it. She said that they were going to meet the guy Gramps had talked about before, this Sudden Sam dude, and that me and Styx should come along.

Now was that cool, because I wanted to see this Sudden Sam but I didn't like the idea of the chicklets arranging everything in The Mouse's life, which they were definitely doing.

So I called Styx and Omega. Omega said he couldn't come. Ceil couldn't come because she had to work in her mother's dress shop. So that left Sheri, Beverly, Styx, and me to go find Sudden Sam.

Now here's where things got a little shaky. Gramps didn't remember exactly where Sam lived, but he remembered that it was near a park in Queens. So we go all the way out to Queens by subway and then to this little park that Gramps knows about.

It's one of those bright, clear days and there are

maybe a trillion and a half kids in the park playing ball and just running around. There are about a trillion and a half dogs running around the park, too. Gramps takes us all the way over to one side of the park behind the handball courts where there aren't many kids, just a few benches and tables.

"We used to sit right there and play checkers," he said. He was pointing at one of those concrete checker tables. "He never could play no checkers. I just let him win once in a while to keep him playing."

"When was the last time you saw him, Gramps?" Sheri asked.

"Must of been—let's see—" He pulled at his chin. " 'Bout some time ago, now."

Great. Styx gave me a look and I gave him one back.

We looked around the park for a while to see if Gramps recognized anything else. He didn't. I saw Sheri was feeling bad so I didn't say anything. We started to leave when Beverly spoke up.

"This Sam guy is old, right?"

"He sure ain't no spring chicken," Gramps said.

"Well, there goes a whole bus of old people."

We looked to where she was pointing and, sure

71

enough, there was a bus across the street from the park and the people getting out of it were all fairly old-looking. I saw the name on the building they were going into. It was the Bartlett Nursing Home.

"That's the place!" Gramps said. "That's where Sam lives."

"A nursing home?" Beverly rolled her eyes up. "He's *that* old?"

"Maybe we should just go home, Gramps," Sheri said.

"I'm all the way out here," Gramps said. "I might as well go and see if Sam is still kicking."

"You mean he might not be?" Styx asked.

"The Lord giveth," Gramps said, "and the Lord taketh away. . . ."

We went over to the Bartlett and a guard stopped us at the door.

"It's okay," Gramps said. "They're with me."

"It might be okay with you," the guard said, "but they don't allow no children in here unless they're relatives of the clientele or get special permission."

So Gramps went in by himself while we all sat around outside.

"Suppose there is a treasure and we do find it," Beverly says. "How are we going to split it up?"

"I got it kind of figured out," Sheri said. "Say there's a million dollars, right?"

"Go on." Beverly was sitting on the ground looking up at Sheri.

"There's three Selects and three guys dancing with us, right? Now, instead of fighting over it I think everybody should get fifty thousand dollars and the rest of the money should go to Gramps and this Sam dude if he's still alive."

"How come Omega is going to get part of the money if he's not helping us to find it?" Beverly asked.

"Okay, so we cut him out," Sheri said.

That was the fastest cut I had ever seen. Omega had lost fifty thousand dollars faster than you could even say the numbers.

We started talking about what we would do with fifty thousand dollars when Sheri sees Gramps coming out of the door. There's this little white guy with him. We all got up as they came over. This guy doesn't look that old from a distance, but when he gets close we could see that his neck was all wrinkled up.

"Kids, this here is Sudden Sam," Gramps said.

"You got a mob with mostly dames in it?" Sudden Sam talked out of the side of his mouth as he looked at the girls.

"Man, this ain't no mob," Gramps said. "These ain't nothing but some kids."

"Yeah, yeah." Sam looked us over. "Let's get somewhere where we can talk business!"

He walked past us toward the park. Sheri made a face and started imitating how Sudden Sam walked, which was sort of a waddle because he was bowlegged. We followed Gramps and Sudden Sam through the park until they stopped at one of the park benches.

"Now let me get this straight," Sudden Sam said. His voice was gravelly. "You want me to help you to find Tiger's dough and then we all split it up between us, right?"

"You got it," Gramps said.

"Well, that's a good idea," Sam said. "I've been thinking about that myself but I need an organization, some troops."

"Did you see that guy on television that was looking for the treasure?" Beverly asked.

"Creep. The guy was a creep," Sam said. "Come on television talking about some kind of mob. We weren't no mob. We were a protection agency. He didn't know nothing. He even come to the Home and talked to me."

"He did?" Gramps asked.

"Yeah. That was before he was on television.

He said he was doing some kind of story, but I didn't trust him none. And I was right, too. Now when Slick here comes in, he levels with me. He's looking for the money. Slick was always an up-front kind of guy."

"Who's Slick?" Beverly asked.

"Who's . . . ?" Sudden Sam looked at Gramps. "What name you using now?"

"I was Slick in the old days," Gramps said. "Now they just call me by regular name, Mr. Jones. How come you wasn't on the television with that fellow if he come here to see you?"

" 'Cause he was gonna cut me out when he found the dough," Sudden Sam said.

An ice-cream truck pulled up just outside the park and a stream of kids started running toward it. Sudden Sam turned to watch them for a while before he went on.

"He wanted to cut me out. That's why he didn't want no television cameras around me. I thought he had it figured out when he found that safe."

"You don't know where the money is?" Gramps asked.

"Got an idea," Sam said. "Tiger, he didn't let anybody know just where anything was, but I got an idea. We got to work out a deal first, though.

I don't open up to nobody unless I got a deal first."

"What kind of deal?" I asked.

"I get twenty-five percent of everything, and I don't carry no heat," Sam said.

"He mean he don't carry no gun," Gramps said, answering our question before anyone asked it.

We looked at each other and at Gramps. No one had thought about carrying a gun.

"How much you figure we can find?" Gramps asked.

"I don't know for sure," Sam said. "But I know there was a lot of talk about Tiger retiring to Paris, France, and living it up big. I got to say three or four million bucks."

"Three or four *million*?" Beverly's eyes got wide.

"So we got a deal?"

"We got a deal!" I said.

"I'm in!" Styx said.

"Gramps?" Sheri looked at her grandfather.

"Sam, things is different than they used to be." Gramps sat on the bench facing Sudden Sam. "These young people don't know nothing 'bout how no gang works. We can't be leading them into no trouble."

"Whaddya think, I don't know what I'm doing?" Sam squinted at Gramps. "I know how they operate these days. They rely on brain instead of muscle. I know that. I ain't stupid."

"Long as you know that, Sam," Gramps said. "Then we got us a deal."

☆

We all get back to the neighborhood and get ready to split to our separate crashes when Beverly calls me to one side.

"Yo, what it is?" The Mouse asked.

"I've just decided that since we going to be part of a gang, I'll be your gun moll," she says. Then she splits, leaving The Mouse standing on the corner with a puzzled look on his handsome mug.

Now what I had to figure out was whether Beverly being my gun moll also meant that she was going to be my girlfriend. That's what I thought she meant but the way I see it, when somebody runs something by The Mouse's ear he hasn't heard before, he's got to find out if they're playing what they're saying or if they're just saying to be playing. The closest thing I had ever had to a girlfriend before was getting stuck with Jennifer Temple as a homework partner to make sure I had done the right pages in the math workbook. With Beverly it was definitely a different set. *Ex-*

citing was the word. Romeo and Juliet. Popeye and spinach. Pork chops and gravy.

Okay. So the next move is when she invites me over to her crash to watch the ball game. We're sitting on the couch. I'm on one side and she's on the other side. We're kind of checking each other out without getting too close. Then The Mouse breaks out with the big question.

"So what would you have said if I didn't want you to be my moll?" I asked.

"Probably broken your face," she answered sweetly.

Okay, so maybe not Romeo and Juliet.

We tubed out a little more and then I said I had to go. I still wasn't sure if the deal was real. She nonchalants me off and starts toward the door. But when we get to the door she puts her arms around my neck, and I knew she was going to kiss me.

Beverly's just a little taller than I am. I was thinking about tiptoeing but I never had a chance. She threw a Dracula lip lock on me that would have sucked my heart out of my body if she hadn't stopped up the top of my lung with her tongue. I was having serious trouble breathing, but I didn't want to let up and look like a lame. So I tried breathing through my nose, but that was getting flattened out in the process. Also, the doorknob was sticking into my back. I was going to be black and blue as well as suffocated.

I opened my eyes and tried to look romantic. But when I opened them I couldn't see anything, she was so close. Then I closed them again and just waited.

The kiss ended just as my eyes were beginning to water and I started seeing these little stars.

"We're going to be really great together," she said. "You're really a good kisser."

On the way home I felt a little tingly. Maybe even a lot tingly. I had kissed girls before, but mostly head kisses. You sort of stand about twelve inches away and kind of lean toward them. That was cool. Even if you kissed them on the lips it was cool. But when you did a whole body kiss topped off by a lip lock it was different. All kinds of things were going on. I didn't think I was in love but I was in something.

Sudden Sam used to know this woman named Katie Donahue, who used to be in the gang, and he figured that if anybody knew where Tiger Moran's old hideout was, she did. He had an address for her out in Queens and we headed out there the following Saturday.

Gramps had an old station wagon he used on his part-time job, which was making deliveries for the drugstore. The Harlem Treasure Crew—which was my name for us—was Beverly, Sheri, Ceil, Styx, me, and Gramps. We all piled into the wagon and went to Queens and picked up Sam and then went to look for Katie Donahue.

"Where did you get this heap?" Sam asked.

Gramps stopped the car and told Sam he could take the train if he wanted to.

"As touchy as you are, you must be getting old or something," Sam said. He smiled his baby-alligator smile.

"Let's get going," Sheri said, heading off the argument.

Meanwhile Beverly's shooting me these glances and The Mouse is embarrassed. I don't even know why I'm embarrassed but I am. Embarrassed and tingly again, even though I'm not even touching Beverly. Maybe it *was* love.

It's a warm day but there aren't too many people on the street once we get off the main drag. The houses we were passing seemed nice though, and I knew that Katie wasn't living in anybody's ghetto.

We had to ask three people before we found the address. We stopped in front of a row of attached houses.

"Maybe we should wait out here in the car," Gramps said. "If she see all of us she might get a little nervous."

"Yeah, maybe," Sam said.

He got out of the car and hitched his pants up. Then he licked his fingertips and smoothed his hair down. He rang the bell and waited.

"The door's opening," Sheri said.

I looked over and saw a young woman standing in the doorway. Sam was talking to her. She just kept shaking her head. There was somebody next to her. It looked like a kid. Then the kid disappeared. I saw Sam take off his hat and nod. Then I saw the kid's face at the window. He was checking us out. I turned back to where Sam was and the woman was shaking her head again. Then Sam started back toward the car and the door closed.

"What happened?" Gramps asked when Sam reached us.

"That was Katie's daughter," Sam said. "Katie passed away about a year ago. The daughter lives there by herself with her boy."

"We might as well get on back home," Gramps said.

It was a downer. We were just about ready to leave when the kid, the same one we saw standing in the doorway, came tearing around from the back of the house. He ran up to us and his face was all red. Now this is the weirdest-looking kid I have ever seen and The Mouse has seen some strange ones, believe it.

"You my grandma's gang?" he asked.

"Who are you?" Gramps asked.

"Gene," he said. "You Grandma's gang?"

"Who's your grandma?" Beverly asked.

"Katie Donahue," the kid said.

"You don't look like no Katie Donahue to me," Gramps said.

Then this weird kid starts walking towards Gramps as big as you please and just walks into him.

Gramps pushed him away.

"Sorry, sir," he said. Then he just stepped away and started staring at us again.

The Mouse decides that this kid is wired weird.

"Somebody better go tell his mama he's loose," Gramps said.

The kid took a watch out of his pocket and started looking at it. Gramps did a double take and checked his wrist.

"Hey! That's my watch!" Gramps said.

"He's got to be Katie's," Sam said.

"Grandma taught me how to do that," the kid says. "In case things got hard."

Okay, so we're standing there looking at this

kid and he's looking at us. Only he looks like somebody put him together with leftover parts. The big thing is that he's got one green eye and one gray eye. If I'm lying I'm flying. He's got bright-red hair and a bunch of freckles, almost as red as his hair, around his nose. And it's all held together with this big grin. He looks like he's been on an island and we just rescued him.

So we're checking him out and he's checking us out. Now everybody is entitled to a glance when they meet somebody new, but this dude's multicolored orbs are inching over us slow and hard. We don't give any slack so we're scoping back, but he holds his ground.

"I know everything about the old gang," he said, finally. "Grandma told me."

"She tell you where Tiger used to hide his money?" Sam took a step toward the kid.

"What's my cut?"

"Say, man, how old are you?" I asked.

"Old enough," the kid shoots back.

I figured "old enough" was about twelve. "How much you want?" I asked.

"Grandma said never take less than ten percent."

"You got it, kid," Sheri said. "Where's the money?"

"It's in a building up in Harlem," the kid said. "And my name ain't kid. It's Eugene."

"What building is it in?" Gramps asked.

"Grandma wasn't sure at first," Eugene said. "She said she and a guy named Tony and Tiger's brother was out in Tony's car one day. Grandma was driving, and they pulled up to a bank that was down from the library, near where the trains run outside."

"Outside?" Beverly looked at me.

"Yeah, that's over there near Broadway," Sam said. "That's where that guy on television looked. Two blocks down from there."

"Grandma said that she and Tony were sitting in the car while Charley Moran went into the bank to get a loan application. Only he came out in a hurry and said he just robbed the bank."

"Yeah! I remember that!" Sam said. "That was Charley Moran. He was always doing stupid stuff to be a big shot, like his brother. He robbed a bank right near Tiger's hideout. Tiger was so mad he hit his brother in the jaw and broke his tooth. We had to lay low for a whole month after that."

"Grandma drove me up there once and we went into the bank and then we got back into the car real quick, just like it was a real bank robbery. She made the same turn and then she went right to the building."

"Where?" We just about all said it at the same time.

"I don't exactly remember," Eugene said. "I think if I went up there again I could find it, though."

"Your mother know anything about this?" Sam asked.

"Nope. Grandma thought she was too square to tell her anything," Eugene said.

"Yeah." Sam was rubbing the side of his chin. "Okay, we'll be in touch with you kid. You just keep it loose, you hear?"

"We going to have special gang names or something?" Eugene asked.

"Sure," Sam said. "We're going to call you Booster. That's a good name for you, kid."

The kid seemed to like that and came up with a big grin.

We all shook hands with Booster and split.

I got the feeling on the way back home that everyone had the same idea. Maybe we were closer to Tiger Moran's loot and maybe we weren't. I had mixed feelings about Booster. On the one hand he was like a little kid who wanted to play games and fool around. On the other hand he was like a little gangster.

"Say, Styx, how much you trust that little dude?" I asked.

"After I shook hands with him I checked my watch and counted my fingers," he said.

There was a lot of watch checking and finger counting on the way home.

Ch-Bop Bop a-Boo-Bop Ch-Bop Bop-a-Boo!
Ch-Bop Bop a-Boo-Bop Ch-Bop Bop-a-Boo!
You can't catch no fish when your line is slack
You can't get no lame to watch your back
When you got to call for your Main Man twice
When your ace ain't high and your cut don't
  slice
When you feel the chill down to your bone
When you dig in the mirror that you all alone
When the good times have slipped away
There is no going back to the yester-way
Ch-Bop Bop a-Boo-Bop Ch-Bop Bop-a-Boo!
Ch-Bop Bop a-Boo-Bop Ch-Bop Bop-a-Boo!

It's Monday and I'm sitting on the back of a park bench half watching a ball game and half thinking about Sam and Gramps and Tiger Moran. Omega is playing with some dudes I don't know and I'm seriously thinking about playing some ball myself. Then this kid with a snotty nose is looking up at me.

"Hey, ain't you the guy the monkey beat?"

"Cop some distance, kid," I said.

"You the guy! You the guy!" The kid had a high voice, even for a kid. He pointed at me and then ran to where some other kids were trying to play basketball with a tennis ball.

A moment later there were five kids around me. One of the older guys at the end of the bench put down his Pepsi and turned to see what was happening.

"He coming again!" the first kid said. His nose was still snotty.

But it was true. They had spotted Pooky and Hollywood coming into the park. Some of the kids ran over to Pooky.

Okay, this is the story. Kids like monkeys. When I was a kid I liked monkeys, too. They're cute and that kind of thing. So naturally they're all excited about a monkey beating a kid playing basketball. Only Hollywood didn't beat me playing basketball. What happened was that Pooky held him *thisclose* to the basket so he could make lay-ups and he made them all. Hollywood wasn't actually playing basketball.

So here comes Pooky and Hollywood. Pooky has put these sunglasses on him and Hollywood keeps taking them off.

All the little kids are running off at the mouth about how Hollywood beat me the last time.

"We heard you was demanding a rematch," Pooky says.

Now Pooky is standing on the court and interrupting the basketball game. But the guys playing the game want to know what's happening and so they come over. Most of the guys playing are older guys, except for Omega.

"Ain't no monkey can beat a human playing basketball," Omega is saying.

"Give me a ball," Pooky calls out.

They give him the ball and he takes Hollywood up to the basket.

Hollywood misses the first basket. Then he makes nine in a row.

"He missed the first on purpose to give you a chance," Pooky said.

He threw me the ball.

"He scared to play the monkey!" the little snot-nosed kid calls out.

"No, he ain't!" another kid answered.

Of course the real deal is that I don't have to shoot against Hollywood. I can just sit down and ignore the whole scene.

"You can't shoot better than a monkey, man?" one of the old guys said.

I started to say something about how I didn't have to get into a contest with a simp chimp, but I saw everybody looking at me and I knew I had to go again. Okay, I was already the talk of the neighborhood with the little kids. I had to shoot down Hollywood to spoil the legend.

I took a deep breath, found my spot on the backboard and put the ball against it.

The first eight shots went right in and then I made a mistake. I looked around and saw the little kids watching me. They were trying to pull the ball out of the hoop with their minds. I'm serious. They wanted that monkey to win. I told myself to stay calm, to keep my arms relaxed. I did stay calm and my arms were so relaxed the ball didn't even reach the backboard. Me and Hollywood were all even with one shot to go. I glanced over at Hollywood and he was sitting on Pooky's shoulder, sunglasses on and a big smile on his face. He thought I was going to miss the last shot.

I took a deep breath and shot harder. The ball rolled around the rim and off the other side.

The sounds all came from behind me as I left the park. I couldn't tell which was louder, Pooky's screaming about how great Hollywood was or everybody else laughing.

But the thing that surprised me was that I didn't feel bad about it. The kids were laughing and I was glad I had missed the last shot. Well, almost glad.

☆

"It's Styx on the phone," Mom said. She had made hamburgers and glanced at them with her don't-leave-before-you-eat look.

Styx said he wanted to see me about something as soon as we could get together. I said okay and downed a hamburger as quickly as I could.

"Is something wrong?" Mom asked.

"No."

"Then why are you in such a hurry?"

"Styx wants to see me about something," I said.

"You shouldn't eat so fast."

"Why not?"

"It could back up on you," she said.

"What does that mean?"

"You know what it means," she answered.

"Oh."

She was a little upset. It couldn't just have been how fast I had eaten, I thought.

"You look a little down," I said.

"Had another fight with your father," she said. "I said all the wrong things."

"You want me to knock him out for you?"

She smiled a sad little smile. I got the feeling that I might get my father back home but it wasn't going to be easy.

I kissed her and went off to check out Styx.

"Did you talk to Sheri?" Styx asked when we had met in front of his house.

"No, what's up?"

"She said that Gramps and Sam were talking and Sam came up with the idea that if Katie went to the bank and it jogged her memory into finding the building, then maybe we could do the whole thing over again with the kid and he would know where to go. We could re-create the whole thing."

"You mean stick up a bank?"

"No, just pretend that we were," Styx said. "He thinks it might jog the kid's memory and he could lead us to where he went with Katie. Sheri says Gramps thinks that Sam knows something else, too, 'cause he's all excited."

"The ride is free," I said. "It don't cost anything to check it out."

"Yeah," Styx said. "But all we know about the original robbery was that Tiger's brother did it, right?"

"Yeah?"

"Well, suppose he shot somebody or something."

Two guys put a box on the sidewalk and put a checkerboard on it.

"Don't be putting no checker setup in front of my house!" a skinny, light-skinned woman called down from the third floor.

"We playing for you, Baby," one of the men, the guy who works in the dry cleaner's, called up to the woman. "Whoever wins get to come up and give you a big kiss right on the mouth!"

"I wouldn't a bit more kiss that evil woman than I would take wings and fly." The other man, Mr. Robinson, who lived in Styx's building, was in his shirt sleeves with a bandana around his neck.

"Why not?" the first man said. "You might as well do something you good at 'cause you sure can't play no checkers!"

"You think something like that happened?" I asked, turning back toward Styx.

"We should check it out," Styx said.

"We could look in the newspapers for the year

she said it happened," I said. The two guys were setting up the checkers.

"There's only one trouble with that," Styx said. "Suppose we find out that they actually did a holdup, right?"

"Go ahead," I said, not really appreciating how smart Styx could be sometimes.

"Then we got to turn them in, right?"

"I don't think there's anybody left to turn in," I said.

"Sam was in the gang," Styx said.

"Oh."

It didn't seem right that something that happened so long ago should get anybody into trouble, I thought. But I could see Styx's point. We had to check things out.

It was really hot and a family across the street had their television up on their fire escape. I looked down and saw an enormous ant crawl over the toe of my sneaker. He probably thought he was a great ant explorer or something. I reached down and flicked him off with my fingernail.

"You want to go to the library with me tomorrow and start looking up bank robberies?" Styx asked.

Then he asked me if I wanted to go over to Sheri's and round up the girls to help. I almost said yes, but then I said no because I wanted to tell him something else.

"They can probably look things up faster than we can," he said.

"Because of Beverly," I said. I couldn't help smiling a little. "We're sort of, you know, doing a Samson and Delilah thing."

"You and *Beverly*?" Styx put his head to one side and looked at me.

"Yeah."

"You went out with her?"

"We were up in her crash," I said.

"You kissed and everything?"

"Yeah. Lip-locked and hung tongues, too."

"What do you mean *and everything*?" he asked.

"I didn't say *and everything*, you did."

"Well, what else you do?"

"I can't tell you everything."

"How come?"

"Because if you're going with a girl you're not supposed to tell everything you do, right?"

"Yeah," he said. "Hey, I didn't know you and Beverly were tight."

"It just happened all of a sudden," I said. "I guess I just swept her off her feet."

"That's why she beat up Bobby Burdette?"

"Probably," I said. I hadn't even realized it at

95

the time, though. I wondered just how long she had been digging me.

Styx had a tennis ball with him. He threw it against one of the wide sycamore trees that line Morningside Avenue. It bounced off crazily and into the street. He didn't go after it or anything. He just watched it go.

"Hey, what did you do that for?" I asked.

"I got to split," he said.

Just like that. He said he had to split and he did. At first I thought he was going after his ball and then he would wait for me, but he didn't. He just left.

Maybe it was stupid. I was adding a little to what happened. I mean, we had lip-locked and it was truly a soul lock, but I had sort of suggested that we did more. I didn't know what Styx thought we might have done, or why he was ticked off. He split so quick I didn't even have a chance to follow him. It didn't make any sense.

I tried to shrug it off on the way home.

Mom was still a little down and she asked me what I wanted to do for the rest of the day. I said nothing and we tubed out together without talking.

We were watching some dumb-butt game show and I was trying to figure out if Styx was mad at me or what. I mean he *looked* mad, but he didn't *sound* mad. I thought about running it past Mom but she didn't look too cool, either.

It rained for a while, one of those sudden showers that come down hard and then they're gone. Soon as it let up Omega called and said they wanted some kids to play ball in the park at seven o'clock.

"It's got something to do with the mayor's office," Omega said. "And everybody gets a T-shirt and we might even get on television."

I wasn't in the mood to play ball but I wasn't in the mood for anything else either, so I said okay. It was seven o'clock when I reached the park. They had turned the lights on and had set up some wooden seats on one side of the courts. The mayor and some people from the police department were there. They were announcing something about how sports could keep kids from getting into trouble.

We were scheduled to play the second game and I went over to where Styx and Omega were sitting.

"What's happening?" I said, sitting next to Omega.

"Nothing much," Omega said. " 'Cept maybe

97

we'll be on television. They said they're gonna shoot a few minutes of each of the games and put the best part on the news tonight."

Styx didn't say anything. I looked over at him and he looked away. I still didn't know what was wrong with him.

The first game was pretty good and the television crews were taping it. The mayor was talking to some people in the crowd and shaking hands.

When the first game ended, a guy from the mayor's office asked who was playing next and Omega said that we were.

"Who's on your team?" this guy asked. He was wearing thick glasses and, I think, a toupee.

Omega pointed out everyone on the team and this guy asked Styx to stand up. When he did and the guy saw how tall Styx was, he asked us to pose with the mayor.

It was hot and Omega was sweating. A girl came over and wiped his face off and put a little powder on him to keep him dry and Omega started grinning. Styx tried to get a smile out but he couldn't seem to make it.

We played and Omega went crazy. He scored nearly every point we made. Styx scored a few baskets. I didn't do that much.

After our game there was one more, but the

mayor left and the television crews left so most of the spectators split, too. I watched part of the next game and then I saw Styx leaving. I let him get almost to the front gate of the playground before I went after him.

"Hey, Styx, wait up!"

He turned, saw that it was me, and nodded.

"Where'd you go this afternoon?" I asked.

"Library," he said.

"I thought we were going tomorrow," I said.

"I went today," he said.

"You find out anything about Katie Donahue, or the bank robbery?" I asked.

"There were a few bank robberies about the time she mentioned," Styx said. "I didn't read anything about anyone being killed, though."

"That's a relief," I said.

"Yeah."

"Hey, man, what's wrong?"

"Nothing."

"Then how come you're acting so funny?"

"What are you talking about?"

"I'm just talking about you acting funny, that's all," I said.

"If you don't like the way I act, don't hang out with me!" Styx said, speeding up his walk.

I ran and caught up with him, taking his arm.

He spun around, put his hand in my face, and started pushing me away. I half swung at his arm and knocked it away from my face. He grabbed me by the neck and pushed me against the fence.

"Who are you pushing, punk?" He had his knee digging into my side. "You want to start something with me?"

"No," I said. At least it was meant to be no. What came out was a strange little noise that didn't sound much like a word.

Styx gave me another push and walked away. I sat down on a park bench and rubbed my neck. It didn't hurt that much or maybe it did, I don't know. I just wondered why he had pushed me like that. I looked up and saw him down the street. He was walking slowly. I didn't know what I was going to do but I got up and went after him again.

He must have heard me coming and he turned around, his fists ready.

"I don't want to fight you," I said. "I just want to know what I did wrong."

"Why are you following me?" he asked.

"I'm following you so you can hit me," I said. "You're my friend and I did something wrong to you, so why don't you just hit me."

"Just don't follow me anymore," he said.

He started off and I followed. He stopped and

looked at me. "You're going to have to hit me," I said. "Either that or tell me what I did wrong."

"Just leave me alone," he said. "Just leave me alone."

I watched my best friend walk away from me. Whoa, it was first-class serious. Styx wasn't being Styx and The Mouse was out in the cold.

—— **8** ——

Boomp! Boomp! Boomp-Boomp!
Boomp! Boomp! Boomp-Boomp!
Your ace is first and your crew is good
But the toughest turf is the neighborhood
If Soul's your goal
You got to come uptown
For the scrapple in the Apple
It's Harlem Town
They got magic cats and get-down dogs
Attitudes and drop-dead Hogs
Light and dark, Black and Brown
The core of the Apple, Harlem Town
Boomp! Boomp! Boomp-Boomp!
Boomp! Boomp! Boomp-Boomp!

We had our first practice with The Selects, but we started goofing through it and Mrs. Bonilla got mad. She was serious about dancing, and I could understand how she didn't dig us making fun of it.

In a way we weren't making fun of the dancing. We just couldn't settle to the metal. She kept showing us what to do and we kept scoping each other. The girls were mad at us, too. We went through the steps for about a half hour and then Mrs. Bonilla called it off. She told us to go home and think about what we were doing.

There was a new flick on One-Two-Five Street and I asked Styx if he wanted to go check it out.

"I don't think so," he said.

"Right," I said.

Ceil and her mama split before the other chicks and I saw that Beverly was waiting for Sheri. I tossed her a winkie and she took my hand.

"Mouse, you guys are going to have to do better the next time we practice," she said.

All the while she's talking there's electricity going up my arm from where she's holding my hand. If you stuck a light bulb on my elbow it would have lit up.

"You want to do some tubing later?" I asked.

"Can't today," she said. "I have to go to the dentist with my mother."

She let my hand go and backed away. There was no doubt about it, my mind was clouded. I wrapped her smile around my heart and floated into the sunset.

☆

"So let me get this straight." Mom's leaning against the sink with a dish towel in her hand. "Sheri's grandfather used to work for Al Capone—"

"No. He worked for Tiger Moran, who was a mob guy about the same time that Al Capone was," I said.

"And this guy in this mob—this Fast Sam—"

"Sudden Sam."

"Okay, this Sudden Sam wants to do something to jog this kid's memory. And this kid's grandmother used to be part of some gang?"

"Yeah, something like that."

"And how old is this kid?"

"About twelve, maybe a little older."

"And for this you swore me to secrecy?"

"Sheri said the treasure could be in the millions," I said. "You want everybody in the neighborhood out looking for it?"

"Don't you think you should talk to your father about this first?"

"What's he going to say?"

"Probably what I should be saying," Mom said. "That you shouldn't be involved with this whole thing."

"Because I'm young, right? And young people shouldn't do anything without having their mothers there, right?"

"I didn't say that." Mom went back to drying the dishes.

"What did you always used to say to me before Mr. D got back into the picture?" I asked. "Didn't you always say when you had a chance for something you really wanted that you should go for it?"

"I'm not so sure now," Mom said. She started screwing up her mouth the way she did sometimes when she was nervous. "And Styx is going along with you on this?"

"Yeah, I guess so. He's ticked off at me for some reason. I think it's got something to do with Beverly."

"Beverly?"

"You remember the girl that came to the house the other night?"

"Yes, she's very pretty."

"Well, we're kind of going together or something," I said.

"You're *going* with her?" Mom put down the

dish towel and sat down. "You have a girl-friend?"

"Hey, it's no big thing," I said.

"You didn't tell me you were dating."

"We're not exactly dating," I said.

"Oh, then you're not really *going* with her," Mom said. She picked up the dish towel again.

"When you kiss like we kiss you're either going together or it's a felony," I said.

Down went the dish towel. "So you're into some heavy kissing?"

"Sort of," I said, spreading it just a little heavier than it was. "I could see I was making her pulse pop a little so I had to make a move before I really wanted to so she wouldn't get frustrated."

"Frustrated?" Mom nodded her head slowly. "Styx doesn't like this girl, too, does he?"

Yo, knockout time. I hadn't thought about it before but Moms was probably right. When I laid the word on Styx I was breaking his heart part.

"You don't have to look so pleased," Mom said.

"I'm not pleased," I said. "I just didn't think about him liking Beverly too."

"As far as this other thing—this treasure—I'd feel a lot better if you and Styx were friends. You guys have been looking out for each other for a long time."

106

"You mean you trust Styx but you don't trust me?"

"No. I mean I trust that if the two of you get into anything that might be a problem, one of you will have enough sense to get you out of it," she said. "Maybe you could put Beverly on hold for a while."

That all sounded reasonable because I was a reasonable kind of guy. But Beverly was probably unreasonable. When a chick really digs a guy, you know, digs him enough to fight for him, then it's not reason, it's passion. When passion is the fashion you just got to step out the way and let the thing cool out. The more I thought of it, there was no way that Beverly could be cool. The Mouse was making her ticker flicker, making her pump jump.

On the other hand, The Mouse was in the saddle with the paddle, on the goal and in control, fit and ready and walking steady. In fact I wasn't even sure if I dug the Beverly person at all. When we had some breeze between us we had some ease between us, but the touch was too much. Her attitude could be rude but her skin was *definitely* in.

I flipped the blip on my psychic radar to full power and saw that if I was going to cool things out I was going to have to work the show through Styx. In fact, there was a chance he was already cooled out.

I called Styx, but his mother said he wasn't home.

"He just took a walk," she said. "Actually, I thought he'd be back by now."

I had started some light tubing when the mother person came into my room. She opened my closet and checked out the floor. The floor of my closet is always a bad point between Moms and me. Mostly because I keep most of my clothes there so I know where they are.

"Mouse, you want to run to the corner and get some soda?" Mom asks.

"Sure."

"You know you're going to have to do something about your closet before school starts in the fall. Right?"

Little digs never hurt The Mouse.

There's a small store a block down from where I live. Mrs. Tice is at the top of the stoop and she's holding her cat, Blackstone, up against her bosom. She's got this expression on her face like she wants to destroy somebody and I see why. Dante Brown, a gentleman of the hoodlum persuasion, is standing at the bottom and he's got this pit bull on a chain.

Now the pit bull is growling and spitting and looking like somebody just said something bad about its mama. And from the way he was pulling at the chain and trying to get at Blackstone it looked like whatever was said was said by a felon feline with a foul mouth.

Meanwhile, guess who is there scoping the public access channel? It's Styx, and he's sitting on the fender of a bad Benz with his peeps on full scope, checking the whole thing out. So I glide over and slide next to him.

"He just want to be friends," Dante's saying. Dante's smiling and showing off his gold. He got a gold chain around his neck, a small gold chain hanging from his ear, and a gold tooth. The pit bull is still straining at his leash with his lips curled back and this low growl coming from somewhere under his chest. He looks like he could chomp down Blackstone with one bite and belch out a perfect meow without losing his appetite.

"You get that beast away from here!" Mrs. Tice is saying. "Before I call the police!"

"Woman, what you gonna call the po-leese on a dog for?" Dante asks. "All he did was to try to make friends with that little rat you got."

"Blackstone is a registered British Black," Mrs. Tice said. "He is not used to this kind of vulgarity!"

"Yeah, but is he tasty?" Dante thought this was really funny.

A small crowd started gathering around and some of the old women started talking about how it was a shame that people could have pit bulls.

"Yeah, why don't you leave her alone?" Check it out: These words came from The Mouse.

Did I tell you that Dante Brown was eighteen feet tall with little muscles on his big muscles? Did I tell you that his pit bull was three feet tall with big muscles on his big muscles and a head bigger than The Mouse's? Did I tell you that when Dante turned to see who had said "Why don't you leave her alone?" my heart skipped three beats?

"Who you?"

"His father is a policeman," Mrs. Tice said. "So go on and bother him. Go on, I dare you!"

Dante looked at me and kind of sneered, and then he chuckled. His pit bull looked at me and kind of sneered, and he chuckled, too. No lie. Then, while I held my breath, they both walked away.

"My father's not a cop," I said to Mrs. Tice.

"That's okay," she said. "You just let him worry about that."

Yeah, right. The crowd broke up and I turned toward Styx. He was smiling.

"You're a tough dude," he said.

"How do I get myself into these things, man?"

"It's your natural macho charm, or something," Styx answered.

"What are you doing over here?"

"I was feeling bad about the argument and stuff," Styx said. "Thinking about coming up to see you."

"Look, man, I didn't peep that you had a thing for Beverly," I said. "I'm sorry."

"A thing for Beverly?" Styx looked at me. "I don't have a thing for Beverly."

"Then how come your jaw turned to cement when I told you we had kissed and stuff?"

It was getting dark and the streetlamps came on. From where we sat on the fender of the car I could see small insects flying around the light globes. Down the street I could see a few people standing on a stoop with their cushions. They would watch the street for a while, then if everything seemed cool they would sit on their cushions and watch the world go by until it was too late to be outside.

"Look, Mouse, I'm sorry the way things went down," Styx said.

"We can deal with it," I said. "We didn't just start running together yesterday."

"Yeah, sure." Styx had one foot on top of the

111

other one. "Remember that time we were going to cut our wrists and be blood brothers?"

"Sure, I remember it."

"You were too chicken to cut your wrist," he said.

"Actually, I was just worried about infection. . . ."

"We don't talk about being friends anymore," Styx said. "Maybe I don't even think about it much but . . . but when you said you and Beverly were friends it made me feel bad."

"Oh."

"I never thought about it before," he said. "It just like, came down on me when you told me about her."

All of a sudden I got the flash. Instant light. I started looking around for something to say.

"Yeah, yeah, I hear you," I said. "Look, I got to do some serious thinking about the whole thing."

I was looking for something else to say, something about understanding how he felt, or at least almost understanding it, when I see this guy running across the street with a baseball bat in his hand. I turned to see what was behind us that he was running toward.

"What you suckers doing on my car?" He stops and starts waving his bat at us.

"We're just sitting here!" Styx said.

"I'm going to break your just-sitting-there heads!" the guy said, and started after Styx. Styx rolled away and ran across the street.

"Stay right there!" the guy's yelling, and swinging his bat in the air. "Don't you move!"

I started up the street with Styx behind me.

"Y'all come back here!"

The guy chased us a half block before stopping and going back to his car.

"I'll see you tomorrow!" I called out to Styx, who was headed down the street to his house.

He raised his fist toward me, the way he had done for as long as I remember. I raised mine back to my friend.

I went to the store and got the soda. I felt really bad about Styx, really bad. I didn't even want to go home.

☆

"What took you so long?"

"I ran into Styx," I said.

"Oh no, I can tell by your face that you two guys didn't make up," she said. "Are you going to cry?"

"The way I feel . . ." The tears were definitely on their way. "Look, is what's-his-name coming by tonight?"

"No, your father isn't coming by tonight," she said. "You want to talk?"

113

"I found out something about Styx tonight," I said. I sat at the kitchen table. "He's gay."

"He told you he was gay?"

"I asked him about what had happened," I said. "And I told him that I was sorry that he had a thing about Beverly."

"What did he say?"

"He said he didn't have a thing for Beverly. He wasn't ticked off about her, he was ticked off about me."

"He told you he was gay?"

"Not really," I said, starting toward my room. "I think I'm going to cop some dreams."

"No, wait a minute," Mom said. "Tell me what Styx said again."

"He said he didn't have a thing about Beverly, and he wasn't ticked about her when I told him. He was ticked about me."

"Mouse?"

"Yeah?"

"How long have you and Styx been best friends?"

"Forever," I said.

"And you think that if you found a new best friend it would still be the same between you?"

"I think he'd understand," I said. "The Styx is a heavy dude."

"I mean, if you told him you weren't going to be best friends anymore, say, next month."

"Why would I say that?"

"Just say that you did."

"He'd feel bad."

"The same way that he felt when you told him that maybe you and Beverly were going to be best friends?"

I looked at the Moms and she had this funny little look on her face.

"You mean you don't think he's—"

"I think he's just worried about your friendship."

How can The Mouse blow? I mean somebody said "Here come the big crunch," and The Mouse thought they said "Hey here come the big lunch," and he left his brain home.

"What should I do?" I asked Mom.

"Did you tell Styx that you thought he was gay?"

"Uh-unh."

"Well, what do you think you should do?"

I get myself together a little bit. What The Mouse felt like was a fool. Like an uncool fool. So I started to go over to Styx's pad and then I thought about something.

"What am I going to say?"

115

"What would you like to say?"

"Hey, I feel like I really love the dude and everything, and I would like to say that, but if I just show up and start running off at the mouth about loving the guy and everything he's gonna think I'm . . . you know."

"He's going to think what you thought?"

"Yeah, he could."

"Don't worry about it, Mouse. He's smarter than you are."

Good thing I was the woman's son or she might really turn me out.

Okay, so the moms person had grounded my flighty psyche and The Mouse was putting a definite chill on the wrong number about my man Styx. Now all I had to do was to Reebok over to his crash and lay out the good news so the boy could rejoice with me.

So I get over and his moms opens the door. She's a senior fox and she thinks The Mouse is about the most charming thing around.

"Hello, Mouse, how are you?" she says. Meanwhile, as she raps out a greeting her hand sort of gestures for me to come on in. A definitely cool move and I store it in my repertoire.

"I'm doing quite well," I say, charmingly.

"Styx is in his room," she said. The hand just

116

turned over and was pointing to my man's room. Definitely the move of a senior fox.

"Yo, my man!"

"Mouse!" Styx said, trying to cover the box of cookies on the bed with a magazine.

"I got a wrong number from what you were saying before," I said, taking several large chocolate chip cookies from the box. "We were rapping about what happened and you said you weren't interested in the chicklet, right?"

"Yeah?"

"I did a delayed double take on that sucker when I got home and I got to thinking that maybe you meant you were liking me or something."

"Like something *what*?"

"I thought maybe you were . . . you know . . . gay or something."

"Yo, man, the last time you took a trip," Styx asked, "did all of you come back?"

"Yeah, man, well, you know all that's good and everything and I said it was a wrong number, but that's not why I'm over here."

"You're over here to do violence to the chocolate chips, right?"

"No, man, I just wanted to tell you that I . . . you know . . . we've been friends for a long time and stuff. . . ."

117

"Yeah?"

"What you mean, *yeah*?"

"I'm just trying to figure out what you're trying to say," he said.

"You know, I mean I don't hate you too much," I said.

"You hate me a little, right?"

The dude was grinning, which blew the whole thing.

"Yo, man, I was going to tell you something nice, but you don't know how to act," I said.

"I didn't say anything," he said.

"Then why you got that grin on your face?"

"I guess I just feel good," he said.

"Why you feel good?" I asked.

"Because my friend came over and said he had something good to tell me," he said.

"Okay, since it made you feel good to know I had something good to tell you, then consider it said, because telling you is not going to make you feel any better."

"Well, I feel the same about you," he said.

"You want to shake on it or anything?"

"What you mean *or anything*?"

So we just sat there for a while and Styx had this stupid grin on his face and I had this stupid grin on my face and we were just sitting and stupid-grinning back and forth. Then The Mouse, being a man of action, decided to get up and give the dude a hug and then split. But when I got up the hug came out like a punch on the shoulder and he gave me a punch on the shoulder.

"You're not too bad for an ugly dude," he said.

Then I split. It wasn't all that I wanted to tell the guy, but if I got more involved than the punch on the shoulder I probably would have had to knock him out completely.

A-Booma-Booma-Booma-Booma Boom Boom!
A-Boom Boom Booma-Booma Boom Boom!
One and one is two—add one for three
But numbers don't make a family
You can smile your smile and grin your grin
But showing teeth don't get you back in
'Cause while you're making up your mind
You're throwing away what's left behind
Fire burns and it sure ain't nice
But it takes a lame to get burned twice
A-Booma-Booma-Booma-Booma Boom Boom!
A-Boom Boom Booma-Booma Boom Boom!

☆

It was time to lobe and globe through a mini-
multi so The Mouse was lying across his bed

120

checking out some new tapes and doing some light tubing while he scoped the current issue of *Heavy Metal* for hidden messages. Then he heard Mr. D backgrounding with the moms person for a while and then he's bruising his knuckles on The Mouse's door.

"Come on in!"

"Hello! It's really loud in here!" he shouts. "Shall I turn something down?"

I shrug and he turns down the sound on the tube and then messes with my tape until he gets the sound down on that.

"There," he says, "that's better."

"Better than what?" I asked.

"How can you hear yourself think in here with all that noise?" he asks.

"I didn't hear the noise because I was in the middle of a mini-multi," I said, hoping he'd notice that he just took the multi out of the mini-multi.

"If I'm doing a mini-multi," I explained, "and I'm on the phone doing my homework with somebody else that's doing a mini-multi, then all together it's a multi-multi."

"Oh . . ." he said. "I just thought I'd come in to see how you were doing."

"That's cool," I said. I put the magazine down. If Mr. D was going to run his lips through some aerobics, I figured he wanted me to hear him.

"I was thinking about getting a job in the area," he said. "What do you think about that?"

"You say a job in the area—you mean a nine-to-five regular slave or a drop-in-once-in-a-while type gig?" I asked.

"I mean a regular job," he said.

"Un-huh. Well, that's the big bomb. What's the fallout?"

"Fallout?"

"Yeah, when you get a local slave, what goes with it? You gonna be trying to deal with Mom again?"

"I had thoughts in that direction," Mr. D said. "I guess the reason I'm talking to you now is that I wanted to know how you felt about it."

"Hey, you're free, brown, and in town so I guess it's your party."

"I'd still like to know what you feel about it, though."

"You're the one on the stage. Don't ask me to dance for you."

He just sat there and I opened the magazine again. I got this feeling inside, it was like somebody had taken a heavy trip, turned it to liquid, and was pouring it into me. The sucker filled me up and by the time Mr. D got up and walked out of the room I thought it was going to overflow.

I got up and turned the tube and the tape back up. I was playing a Golden Oldie called "Purple Rain" and it hit the mood just right.

I couldn't get the words from the magazine past my eyes into my brain so I closed it. The tube went in through the back way, skipping the think mode, which is righteous when you got your think box clogged up with other junk.

The Road Runner was beep-beeping across the screen. I had scoped the set before but I watched it anyway. The coyote had been blown up and electrocuted and had fallen off two cliffs by the time the moms person came rapping.

I didn't scope her at first and then I did and saw that she had tears in her eyes. All I wanted to do was to tune back to the tube, but I knew that wouldn't do. I flicked the remote and watched the coyote take the ultimate fade, then turned down the tape again.

"So, what it is?"

"He tell you about getting a job in the area?"

"Yeah," I said.

"He said you weren't very happy about it."

"You going to deal with him again?"

"He wants to try."

"What do you want?"

"I don't know." She sat down on the edge of the

123

bed. "I'm a little nervous about it. I want to and I don't. You know what I mean?"

"That's the way I feel," I said. "You know, when something happens that's cool and not cool at the same time, you look for a way to make it . . . what?"

"Not so risky?" She was starting to cry.

"Yeah. Hey, don't cry! You're going to have me watering *my* nose."

"Go on, tell me what you're thinking," she said. "I really need to know."

"That's what it is," I said. "All this time I've been dealing without the dude and sometimes, like, it's been sticky. But I got all my moves in place. If somebody asks a question about where my father is, I got about nine steps I can do, depending on who's popping the Q. If I thought he was going to do a magic number and make things all right, then it would be different. But it was too hard learning all the my-father-don't-live-here moves just to give them up on a humble."

"A humble?"

"I don't mean the dude's not sincere and stuff," I said. "But if you didn't think he was sincere the first time you Ping-Ponged into the deal, you wouldn't be thinking about picking up the paddle again."

"That's the way I feel, too," she said. "But at the same time . . ."

"You want to check it out—"

"I think so."

"Well"—I put my hand on hers—"I guess you can call me Jack Horner, 'cause I'm definitely in your corner."

"Thanks, Mouse." The mother person patted me on my hand. "I'm not sure what's going to happen, but I think we feel the same way. And I'm glad you're in my corner."

"Whose corner I'm gonna be in if not the Champ's?"

"Right on!" she said, and left the room.

Right on? What was that supposed to mean?

Anyway I had to get down some new moves. I had to break it to Styx and the crew that Mr. D might be attempting a comeback.

Personally, The Mouse thought the dude had a lot of nerve. He must have held the words in his mouth for a week trying to spit them out. It's a wonder he didn't choke on them. But I could see where it might be together if he slid back in. Maybe not so much for The Mouse, but I thought the moms person could dig it.

Sheri called. "We've got a problem," she said.

"Go on."

125

"Gramps was talking to my mother this morning," she said. "And from what he was saying I'm getting the feeling that he wants to forget this looking for the money. I think he's a little leery of Sam, and the kid doesn't help."

"The kid is the tip," I said. "Gramps was always on the edge of this thing, but when the kid came on the scene he tipped him over."

"Maybe we should just give it up," Sheri said.

Now The Mouse did not want to give up the look for the loot. In the first place having a lot of cash in your stash is better than having a sharp stick in your eye. Second, if we found the bucks, we could get famous. Third, and most important of all, it was something to do.

"Good." I had slipped my brain into warp drive. "That gets us out of dancing, too."

"Mouse, don't be like that," Sheri said. "Look, let me see what I can do."

"Are you down for bringing the kid to the neighborhood?" I asked. "We can school the fool and let Gramps dig him again."

"I don't think it's going to work," Sheri said. "Gramps just don't like the little sucker."

"You got another idea?"

There was a long pause. "How we going to get him up here?"

"I'll meet him someplace and bring him on up."

"Suppose he doesn't want to come?"

"Then we can get us a Chinese checkers tournament or something else to do. I don't know."

Sheri wasn't thrilled by The Mouse's plan, but it was the only one we had. I Touch-Toned the operator, gave her the address, and asked her for the number of Kate Donahue. The operator checked it out and said that she didn't have a Kate Donahue listed.

"We have a B. Donahue," she said.

"May I have that, please?" I said. I figured that might have been the kid's mother's name.

The operator went off and this mechanical voice came on and gave me a number. I wrote it down, crossed my fingers, and made the call.

"The Donahues'!" The dude announced it in this real deep voice like the Donahues were going to break into a dance number or something.

"Look, man, this is Mouse."

"Is this Stinky?" He slipped into his kid's voice.

"Stinky? No, this is Mouse . . . you know, from Katie's gang."

"Oh, hi." My man was back to his deep voice. "This is Booster."

"Look, Booster, how would you like to come up to Harlem and see what the rest of the gang does when we're not ganging around?"

Silence.

"Hey, Booster, you there?"

"Sure. I'll come. How do I get there?"

"I'll come and pick you up," I said. "You sure your mother will let you come?"

"No problem," he said. "She goes to work at twelve o'clock. But I got to be back home at five minutes past seven. That's when she calls to find out if I'm okay and stuff."

"Bet! I'll be there." I said.

10

Cut on down, Bam Bam! Cut on down!
Cut on down, Yeah Slam! Cut on down!
Don't call me down 'til you know my name
Don't play me cheap 'til you catch my game
Don't dis me down to cop my flash
Don't flash your slice to keep me cool
Don't pull no piece and play me fool
Don't fool with me I ain't no sap
I'll Reebok home and end this rap
Cut on down, Bam Bam! Cut on down!
Cut on down, Yeah Slam! Cut on down!

I called Styx and we took the magic dragon out
to Queens to pick up Booster. It was the second

of July and hot. When we got off the dragon in Queens we saw this woman selling cold drinks and we bought two apiece and drank them as we Reeboked to Booster's crash. So what does my man have on when me and Styx pick him up? He's wearing this long coat that comes down below his knees.

"You expecting rain or something?" Styx asked as Booster locked his front door.

"Never can tell," Booster says. And he says it cool like, like he's Sudden Sam. The kid is definitely into the part.

"How come you can pick pockets like that?" I asked when we had reached the dragon again. "I know your grandma taught you, but did you really practice and everything?"

"When my father died, Grandma said I had to have something to fall back on. In case I didn't go to college."

"You going to college?"

"Never can tell."

"How did your father die?" I asked. I really didn't want to ask because I figured he had either been shot by the police or rubbed out by the mob and dropped in the river.

"He got hit by a car," he said.

"Oh."

"Brown."

"Right."

We got Booster up to Harlem and took him to the park. He didn't say a word but he watched everybody. A couple of dudes were watching him, too. Styx went to call Sheri and I told the kid about the plans.

"Look. Gramps is getting a little shaky about making believe we're going to rob a bank and everything," I said. "I think he's a little shaky about you, too. So what we want to do is to run you by his place so that he can see that you're a regular guy. Okay?"

"Who's Gramps?"

"You took his watch, remember?"

"Okay."

"And don't go picking anybody's pockets," I said. "And if you have any other little nasty habits, be cool with them, too."

He gave me a look and I could see he was digging the whole scene. In his mind he was this big-time hood from Queens trying to cut the mustard in the toughest gang in New York. Maybe even the whole East Coast.

Styx came back and said that Sheri said they wanted us to come by her place and try out the dance. Styx said he was going to go ahead and me

131

and Booster should come a few minutes later so that it wouldn't look like a planned thing.

I get there with Booster and I see Omega and Styx are there wearing basketball uniforms. I think maybe I missed something about a game, but I find out that Ceil's mother has this whole new dance we're supposed to do.

"It's like basketball," she says. "Do we have another dancer?"

She's scoping Booster, who definitely doesn't look like a dancer. So Booster parks himself, in his long raincoat, on the couch and does his hard-stare number while I'm changing into this basketball uniform Ceil's mother has come up with.

Meanwhile, Gramps is in the kitchen, but he keeps going past the door where we are so he can see what's happening. By the time I get out of the bathroom in the basketball uniform I catch a serious case of the giggles.

Things were going to work out. Gramps would see the guys practicing the dancing and would notice that Booster was just checking everybody out and wasn't getting into anything weird.

"So what's this dance about?" I say.

"It's like basketball," Mrs. Bonilla says in this don't-worry-about-it voice.

What, I asked myself, does a lady from Mexico

know about the royal game of basketball? From whence does she get her poop on the hoop? I know a lame can't dig the game so the whole thing has to make a steady drift into Bustville, right?

Okay, hit the gong because The Mouse was wrong. She don't know the rules but she got all the moves. She had us hipping and dipping more than we did on the court. The Mouse was moving and grooving to a salsa beat, shaking and baking in the summer heat. The Styx is sweet and Omega's mean, they're throwing down steps I'd never seen.

The whole thing was like a game. First Omega, Sheri, and me were on one side against Styx, Beverly, and Ceil, then we paired off with two against two.

Now we had to keep one eye on Ceil's mama, who was mostly showing us what to do and we had to figure out where we were supposed to be. The whole thing was on the money for about five minutes. Then I got the feeling that Omega and Styx were trying to outdance Numero Uno.

So I'm ready to get serious, but the wagon is dragging because dancing is harder than ball! I'm looking for some bench time and some oh-two. Then I check out Beverly's eyeballs dribbling over in my direction and I suck in a heavy breath and keep on keeping on. The Mouse has got little spots floating in front of his eyes and is steady pumping his arms trying to catch up with the beat.

"One boy with each girl! One boy with each girl!" Ceil's mother is still going strong. I wind up in front of Beverly or maybe she wound up in front of me. She's wearing shorts, the same as me, and there's sweat on her legs. What I could see through the sweat in my eyes looked good.

Okay, so we go through the dance and then we got to go through it again. Then we did it one more time. We did us one more one more time and then two more one more times after that. When we finally finished, my sweat was so tired I had to throw it on the floor because it was too tired to roll down my arm and get there itself.

One good thing come out of all this. Gramps is checking it all out and he thinks it's the stupidest thing he's ever seen. He looked at me, Styx, and Omega and he laughed. Then he looked over at Booster sitting on the couch with his coat on and he laughed at that. The dude was having a good time.

Ceil's mama didn't let us go until Styx got a cramp in his hamstrings and couldn't dance any-more. If I had known it was that easy I would have put a knot in mine twenty minutes after we had arrived.

"What do you think, Gramps?" Sheri asked.

"The *girls* looked okay," Gramps said.

Sheri went and put her head on his chest. He looked at us and smiled. Okay, we had him.

What I wanted to do was to go home, pour myself into bed, and put myself on serious pause for about fifty years. What I had to do was to make sure that Booster got back to his crash.

Styx couldn't make it. In fact he could hardly walk, and Ceil and Beverly were going to help him home. I gave Beverly a little wink and started off with Booster.

"I don't need you to go with me," he said. "I've been in the city plenty of times by myself."

I leaned over to him and spoke in my Jimmy Cagney voice. "As long as you got the key to where the loot is, I got to make sure nothing happens to ya, kid."

We copped the magic dragon and took it down to Forty-deuce, where we switched over to the Queens train. The whole thousand miles out to Queens where Booster lives he's rapping about how we can stay together even after we finish the job and how we can do other jobs together.

"Like what?" I asked him.

"Say, if the United States wanted something secret out of the U.N. and needed somebody to go down and steal it," he said.

"They got the C.I.A., the F.B.I., and three vowels they ain't even used yet and they going to call on us?"

"You never can tell," he said.

"Say we get the money," I said to him, "and it comes to a million dollars apiece, what you going to do with yours?"

"Buy the St. Louis Cardinals," he says, with as serious a face as you can get with one green eye and one gray eye, "and then send them off to Africa or someplace 'cause I hate them!"

"Well, okay. I know a monkey you can send with them," I said.

We got off at Willets Point. Willets Point is about five blocks from where Booster lives and right near Shea Stadium, the home of the Mets. There wasn't a game so not many people got off there.

"Yo! My man, you want a Mets cap?"

I turned and saw a guy with a shopping bag. He reached into it and pulled out a blue Mets cap.

"I don't think so," I said.

"They're cheap today," he said. "Two dollars."

136

Now, I know baseball caps cost more than two dollars. I see the guy looking around and the way I figure it, he must have stolen the caps. No way I'm going to buy a stolen cap even though I've been a Mets fan most of my life.

"That's pretty cheap," Booster says. He takes the cap and puts it on me.

"There ain't many customers around is why I'm selling them so cheap," he said. The guy is still looking around and I think he's looking for other customers. There aren't any because the train platform is deserted.

"I still don't think I want one," I said, trying to maneuver around the guy.

Then he gave me a shove backward and pulled out a blade about a half foot long.

"Okay, give up the cash, sucker!" he said, waving the knife in front of him.

Booster started going under his coat and swishing himself around and I'm checking him out. I just hope he didn't take a lot of money from home. But he don't pull out any money. He pulls out the biggest pistol I have ever seen in my whole entire life!

"You get away from here!" he said. He's got his green eye almost closed and his gray eye is peeping down the barrel.

"That gun ain't real," the guy said, looking at me. "Is it?"

Booster pulled back the hammer. "You know any prayers, you better say 'em quick!" he said.

The guy backed off about two quick steps, then dropped the bag of caps and took off. Only he ran the wrong way because there wasn't any exit at that end of the platform. He ran to the end of it, realized what he had done, then stopped and turned back toward us.

"Let's get out of here," I said to Booster.

"You think I should shoot him?"

I looked at him and he's looking serious, then he gave me this little hurt smile. "Only fooling," he said. "Only fooling."

We got the gun back under his coat and got out of there as soon as we could. The Mouse held his breath from the time we got off the platform all the way to Booster's house.

"Look, man, let me share something with you. I hate you," I said calmly. "You're going to fool around and get me killed."

"Just a minute. I gotta go—" he said.

He ran upstairs and I just shook my head. There was bad news and bad news. This kid was a telegram with a black border. I heard the toilet flush and he came down again.

"Look, Booster—"

138

"That guy thought the gun was real, huh?"

"It was real," I said.

"No way," Booster said. "No way. I'm not a stickup guy."

"Yeah, right."

The phone rang. I looked up at the clock. It was seven oh five. I headed for the front door as Booster headed for the phone.

No matter what Booster said, I thought the gun was real. That's the first thing. The second thing was that it really didn't matter if it was real or not. What did matter is that I had to decide if I wanted to run around with some crazy kid who thought he was Al Capone, Jr.

The thing was that I still wanted to look for the treasure if there was one. Also, I wanted to have something to do while my moms and Mr. D did whatever number it was they were going to do. What I decided to do was to keep my eye on Booster. I would personally make sure that the little dude wasn't carrying any guns, knives, or stealth bombers under his coat.

I flashed to my crash and stamped the drain in the indoor rain.

"A certain young lady called," Mom said when I had got out of the shower.

She's wearing this I-know-all-about-it look on

her face so I know it has to be Beverly. Then she hands me a twenty-dollar bill.

"What's this for?"

"She mentioned something about a movie that she thought you might want to see."

"When did she call?"

"About six thirty," Mom said. "How did it go with the dancing? I saw Mrs. Jones in the market and she told me she thought it went all right."

"Okay," I said. "A little rougher than I thought it would be, but nothing I can't handle."

"Beverly something you can handle?" she asked. She didn't wait for an answer. She just gave me a foxy look and waltzed into the kitchen.

Okay. I called Beverly and she said that she thought she heard me mention that I wanted to see the movie playing over at the Loew's State. As a matter of fact I had wanted to go see it, but I had kind of planned to go with Styx. But I had the money so I figured I would give Beverly a break.

Okay. Now The Mouse has been doing a Snow White, checking himself out in the marvelous mirror of his magnificent mind, digging the B side of his own soulful psyche, and checking out the motives behind his moves. And as far as Beverly was concerned the motives behind the moves were the motion of her oceans of outrageous parts. And it wasn't just the eyes that were scoping, it was something deeper than eyes that was scoping and hoping and roping The Mouse into an amorous schizofrenzy. And if it wasn't true love it would have to do until the true came through.

The movie was *The Son of Rambo, Part III.* It's where Rambo Jr. and Michael Myers team up for the first time.

Anyway, I'm in the movie with Beverly, going over my plans to put my arm around her.

"Why don't you put your arm around me?" Beverly said.

Was that a hint? Yeah. Okay.

Now I know you're supposed to lip lock in the movies, right? Only I remember the last lip-lock session so I'm a little nervous. Not Beverly. Different locale, same gal. Same lip, same trip. We missed all the coming attractions. Beverly didn't cool down until the movie started.

Did I tell you this was a Friday-night bash? It was. When I got home I felt like I had run a marathon. I eased into some zzzz's and didn't bring the lids to half-mast until deep in the A.M. when the moms person woke me with the news.

"Styx is on the phone," she said. "You ready for breakfast?"

"I'm ready," I said. I got the remote, zapped on some 'toons, and picked up the phone.

"Guess who called me yesterday?"

"Who?"

"Beverly."

"Beverly?"

"Yeah, she called just after six, must have been right after she and Sheri helped me home. She asked me if I had a girlfriend," Styx said. "I said no and she asked me if I wanted her to be my girlfriend."

"She asked you *what*?"

"Yeah. So I said I thought she probably already had a boyfriend and she said she didn't. Then I said I didn't want a girlfriend."

"She said she didn't have a boyfriend?"

"Yeah," Styx said.

"That's weird."

"You can say that again. Look, you going to play ball today?"

"Yeah, I guess so."

I told Styx I would meet him in the park and started getting ready. Yo, man, Beverly was on my brain. It was her idea that I was going to be her boyfriend, not mine. I couldn't figure out what she was doing.

Maybe it was just that I didn't want her to ditch me for Styx.

I don't know, maybe I did like her or something. I knew I didn't want to see Styx. On the other hand, I didn't want to act like it was tearing me up or anything.

I thought about laying it on the moms person to see what she thought about it, but I didn't. I just felt too bad to talk about it.

Whoop! Whoop! Chum-Chummmm
Whoop! Whoop! Chum-Chummmm
Yo! My name is Mouse and I'm Mr. Cool
And I'm gonna whip some big-time fool
Big got to stall and big got to fall
Big got to hear that losing call
Big got to sigh and big got to cry
Old got to hit the road and fly
He's a no-stick no-kick slow-hopping fool
Facing fast-moving slow-grooving sweet Mr.
  Cool
Whoop! Whoop! Chum-Chummmm
Whoop! Whoop! Chum-Chummmm

☆

So now I got a big mad at Beverly for chumping me off on the QT, a little mad at Styx for telling me about it, and a medium-sized mad at me for not telling Styx that I was mad at everybody. So what I was going to do was to ignore the whole thing. Turn the deal around and go from a fool to aloof. Put my mind on remote and channel in the park. Maybe the sports channel. Rock and jock a little. Shoot some hoops, work up a little sweat.

Toast is in the park and he, Styx, and I team up against these three guys we didn't know. They had a little game going and they were playing us tough, but that wasn't good enough for them. They wanted to kangaroo us. Jump up in our faces and down our throats. The way they thought they were going to do that was to push us around. They weren't taller than us, but they were heavier.

The guy playing against Toast was maybe in his twenties. The guy playing against Styx wasn't that old but he was tough-looking and every time he missed a shot he started polluting the air with the alphabet words. First he'd start with the *S* word, then switch to the *F* word, and then run down the rest of the *'BC*'s.

The dude I was holding looked like a fugitive from Halloween. Instead of sweatbands he should

145

have been carrying around a trick-or-treat bag. He was big and slow and his breath smelled like something had died and he was holding it in his mouth until he had time to bury it. The way he was guarding me mostly was holding my wrist so I wouldn't get away from him. What the set amounted to was three young cats—me, Styx, and Toast—playing against three old guys who ran their mouths better than they ran their game.

Now, my man Toast don't take too much pushing and shoving and before you know it there's a big argument going on. Toast and this guy are toe-to-toeing and I'm checking it out to see if they're going to fight. Then Styx's man gets into the act and starts mouthing off and putting his finger in Styx's chest. Styx pushes him away, not even too hard, but the guy falls down.

"Fight! Fight!" two little kids started screaming.

Then who shows up but Bobby Burdette.

"Y'all better cool out before Mighty Mouse gets mad," he calls out. "He get mad he gonna run home and get his woman to whip your head!"

Now, I was the only one who wasn't mad at anybody, right? So who gets hit? Me.

The guy I was holding hits me once in the

stomach and then swings about four more times, but he misses. I back up and look at him and he's circling around me and breathing hard and looking as mean as he can look, which is pretty mean.

He swings at me again but he keeps missing. That's because his feet get near to me but he's leaning his body way back so he don't get hit.

"You better go get your woman!" Burdette is calling out.

"Knock him out!" The guy who was arguing with Toast is sitting down on the bench and watching Bad Breath coming after me.

Why, I ask myself, is all this violence entering The Mouse's life? Before I can answer myself old Bad Breath is swinging at me again. I swing back at the guy and I miss. Then he swings twice and he misses. So far so good. I got real close and tried to hit him and I missed again and this time I fell forward. He hit me on the top of the head and I fell down.

I looked up and saw him coming around to hit me while I'm down. I'm in trouble because this guy is as big as King Kong's daddy. So I kicked him on his leg.

Bam! He went down. Just like that. I rolled over and got up. He was still lying on the ground. His leg is sticking out at a right angle. The Mouse is hip to the fact that legs are not supposed to stick out at no right angles.

"Oh, sweat!" This comes from a mini-chicklet on the side. "He broke his leg with a karate kick!"

Everybody is looking down at this guy laying on the ground. We watch as he sits up and starts fumbling with his leg. He didn't look like he was in a lot of pain or anything. Then I see him pull his leg out from his pants. The sucker is artificial. No wonder he couldn't keep up playing ball.

He pulls his leg out and it's got these straps on it. He's not saying anything and everybody is checking him out with their mouths open because we've never seen anything like this before. Then he wrapped one end of the straps around his hand and started swinging it like a sling. *Pow!* Right in my eye. I get kicked in the eye by a leg that's not even hooked on to a dude.

I tried to grab his leg when he swung it again. It hit my hand and that hurt, too. I got it the next time he swung and kicked at him. He was still on the ground and I got him on the shoulder. The shoulder didn't come off.

The dude snatched his leg back and started swinging it over his head. There was only one brave thing to do and I did it. I ran out of the park.

I didn't turn around until I hit the street. I'd call Styx later.

By the time I got home my eye was starting to swell. I could still see those little stars you get when you hurt your eye. Mr. D was there, which was a trip. Normally Mom would have run over to me and asked me what was wrong and maybe gone a little crazy. Which is one of the good jobs that moms have. But with Mr. D around she was trying to be supercool and everything so she just lays this little question on me.

"Something in your eye?"

"I got kicked in it," I said.

Silence.

"Kicked?"

"This guy was sitting on the ground swinging his leg over his head, see. . . ."

It seems Mr. D was at the house because he and Mom were going out on a date. Whatever they had argued about I guess they had made up. He asked me how he looked. I didn't even care how he looked. Mom looked nice.

"I'd put some ice on that eye if I were you," Mr. D says.

Mom is still being cool but she pats my hand as she's telling me where the hamburgers are. She's worried about my eye. Good.

They had split about thirty minutes before and I had just settled down to some one-eyed tubing when the phone rang. Sudden Sam.

"You come up with anything yet?"

"Like what?" I asked. I saw myself in the mirror. The eye was going to be black.

"To jog the kid's memory."

"I thought we were going to try to find the bank and go through the same steps that he and his grandma went through before," I said.

"Yeah. Yeah," he said. "You got a good head on your shoulders, Rat."

"Yo, it ain't Rat. It's Mouse."

"Well, you still got a good head on your shoulders," Sam said.

"I'm pretty swift," I said.

"When you going to do it, this week?"

"Might as well."

"We ought to stage it like it's the real thing," Sam said. "The kid'll get all excited and maybe it'll trigger something. Maybe if we plan it so he's got a part we don't even have to do it. It'll just come to him in a flash."

"That would really be cool," I said.

"You'd better call the rest of the guys and let them know what your plans are," Sam said. "Especially Slick. Sometimes I think he's a little shaky. You think he's getting old or something?"

"He's all right," I said. "I'll call him first."

"Good," Sam said. "That's probably the way I would have handled it if I was leading this outfit."

So Sam had another idea and wanted me to go along with it. Okay, that was cool. It was also cool for him to try to make me think it was my idea. I dialed Sheri's house and got Gramps.

"It ain't going to work!" Gramps' voice was strong on the phone. "I don't think anything's going to jog that kid's memory because I don't think he knows anything!"

"If he sees the same bank and the same streets he saw before . . ." I started saying.

Gramps cleared his throat a few times and I heard him talking to Sheri. After a long while he said he would go along with it, but he didn't like it none.

I called Styx and told him about the idea. Styx said it sounded okay to him.

"How's your eye?"

"It's going to be a little swollen."

"After you left, that guy found out that his foot was broken," Styx said. "The one he hit you with."

"Serves him right."

We talked a little more and I asked him to call Beverly and tell her about the new plan. I didn't want to talk to her. So who calls me an hour later just when I'm putting one of those popcorn packages in the microwave? Right.

"You think the idea is going to work?" Beverly asked.

"I don't know," I said, casually.

Silence. She didn't say anything and I didn't say anything in return. Then she asked if I was mad with her.

"Why should I be mad with you?" I asked.

"Styx told me that he told you I asked him if he wanted to be my boyfriend," she said. "I thought maybe you were getting too serious."

I was getting too serious? Who was asking *who* out? Who was throwing around all the heavy lip locks?

"So are we through, or what?" I said.

"Well, if you promise not to get too serious," Beverly said, "you can still be my boyfriend."

12

Hummm-Hm! Hummm-Hm!
Hummm-Hm! Hummm-Hm!
The Mouse got the gift, he's the mighty Rover
When you're getting by, he's getting over
But getting down don't mean no ground
And a get-over don't keep The Mouse around
'Cause the Mouse don't play nor does he joke
When it's time to go he goes for broke
He can shake, he can bake, but you know he
  ain't fake
He can wheel, he can deal, but you know he
  don't steal
Hummm-Hm! Hummm-Hm!
Hummm-Hm! Hummm-Hm!

Sam calls me first thing Monday morning and says that maybe somebody should go and look over the bank.

"Case it," he said.

"Why?" I asked. "We're just going in to look around and see if Booster remembers anything."

"I thought we were going through the whole thing," he said. "You know, going in and then riding away from the bank like we were trying to get away or something."

"Yeah, I guess so," I said.

"You ain't got the stomach for it, right?" Sam said. "I told Slick you kids would get bored with it. The money don't mean nothing to you guys anyway."

"We're not bored," I said. "I don't mind looking the bank over."

"You want me to go along with you?" Sam asked.

"I can case the joint," I said. "Maybe I'll do it tomorrow."

The first thing I thought about was Touch-Toning the Styx and asking him to go along with me. Then I remembered the Beverly bit and changed my mind. Then I changed my mind again. I'd give him a call just to show that it didn't mean anything to me.

I picked up the phone to dial and nothing happened. My fingers didn't work. It just wasn't easy calling Styx. It had something to do with Beverly, about her being a chicklet and everything. Styx and I were against each other even though neither of us wanted to win. I even got the feeling that maybe that was why Beverly was dealing the way she was. Maybe she didn't want to be my girlfriend or Styx's, or anybody's moll. Maybe she just dug having people sweat over who was who. The Mouse definitely was going to have to check out his Webster's to see if any of those definitions like boyfriend, and girlfriend, and main squeeze, had changed when he wasn't looking.

I decided to case the bank myself that afternoon.

The bank was no big deal. It was one of those old, really big banks that took up nearly the whole end of the block. Over the front door there was a large gold clock with old-fashioned numbers. When I got inside, though, everything was pretty modern. There were two of those machines where you get instant cash and a stand that had a lot of brochures and some tax forms.

On one side there were desks with people sitting at them. I think they were the people you had to go to if you wanted a loan or anything.

On the other side, nearer the door I walked in, were the tellers. There was a side entrance. I went around to that, and that side had two more of those instant cash machines, a long table with a glass top, and a telephone. It looked like just about every bank I had been in. Like I said, no big deal.

I thought about drawing a picture of the bank, but I didn't see any real reason. I wasn't thinking about the bank that much. What I was still thinking about was Styx and Beverly. My pockets were full of change and I went over and stepped into the phone booth. I was going to try to call Styx one more time. Maybe talk things over the way we used to.

The second dime had just dropped when I looked up and saw somebody come into the bank that I thought I recognized. He went behind a pole for a moment. I watched until he came around the other side. It was Sudden Sam. The guy didn't trust me. He was casing the bank himself. I thought about hanging up right away and going over to him but I didn't. I dialed Styx's number instead.

"They're making a big deal of the whole thing," Styx said over the phone. "Sheri said that Gramps was talking about it again, too."

"I didn't think he was that hot on finding the treasure," I said. "He started it and all but I thought he was kind of cooling out on it."

"Well, we'll know one way or the other soon enough," Styx said.

"Yeah, look." I traced my finger along the edge of the telephone. "Hey, look, I talked to Beverly again."

"Yeah?"

"We're probably still going to be . . . you know."

"I don't think it should be a big deal with her though," Styx said. "You've got to be cool."

"I know what you mean," I said, glad to have at least brought up the subject.

"Sam still casing the place?" Styx asked.

"Yeah." I watched Sam move around the bank and told Styx what he was doing. I turned my back to Sam when he looked over toward the telephone booth and I didn't know if he saw me or not. When I turned around again he was gone.

After I hung up the phone I left the bank. I stopped down the street near the George Bruce Library and bought a package of mints. I thought more about Styx. We had talked okay, and he seemed friendly enough, but there were times when it wasn't like before. Even if it was Beverly that was messing around with our minds, it still felt as if I were competing against Styx.

Thursday morning. I thought Thursday was

going to be a good day for all of us to go to the bank. When I woke up the sun was shining. I'm feeling good and Mom is feeling good. I can tell she is because she's making coffee when I get to the kitchen and she's singing. She sings off-key but it's cool.

"You have a big day planned?" she asks.

"We're going to walk Booster through the bank thing," I said. I didn't want to get into too many details about it.

"How old did you say he was?" Mom was putting plates on the table.

"I'm not hungry," I said.

"You're not eating for you," she answered. "You're eating for me. You eat so I feel good."

"If I eat too much for you will you gain weight?"

"I'd better not," she said. "Don't forget to check the mail before you leave, okay?"

Mom ate the way she always did, in a hurry and mostly standing up. Then she gave me a kiss with crumbs on her mouth and left for work. Love them crumb kisses.

She's out the door maybe a minute, maybe two when the phone rings. It's Mr. D and he wants to talk to Mom. I tell him that she's already gone and he's disappointed. Then he says he's thinking about taking the day off and wants to know if I want to "hang out."

"Nope."

"So what are you doing today?"

"Hanging out with the guys," I said.

"Oh."

I didn't mean it that way, not the way it sounded. I tried to think of something to say, and then he said he'd give me a call later and hung up.

Actually I was getting used to having the guy around. He was okay, really. I even liked him trying to cop some relationship. But that was part of the problem, too. Sometimes things you want in life come with little price tags on them that read "risk" and "not sure" and "confusion." The Mouse didn't want to give up anything. He didn't want to give up Mom to get Dad back, or Beverly so he'd be cool with Styx again. The thought made The Mouse feel a little like Queasy Glider, so he Reeboked his psyche in the direction of the tube, where it was always safe from thoughts, good, bad, or otherwise.

When I got to Sheri's house where we were supposed to meet there was a small crowd gathered. What they were looking at was the ancient-looking car that Sam was leaning on.

"What is that?" I asked.

"This here's a Packard," Gramps said. "I borrowed it from a friend so we can do this thing in style. They don't make them like this anymore."

I could see why they didn't. The thing was enormous with huge headlights and a spare tire on the outside of the back. But somebody had taken good care of it, because it was spotless.

"Where's the star?" Sheri asked, referring to Booster.

"Styx is picking him up," I said. "I told them to wait for us at the subway on St. Nicholas."

"Well, let's get this show on the road," Sam said.

We all piled into the Packard and I thought we probably looked like a circus act or something.

I was the first to spot Styx and Booster standing on the corner at St. Nicholas and remembered what had happened with my man before.

"Hey, let me check out Booster, make sure he doesn't have to go to the bathroom or something. I don't want to be jogging his kidneys when we're supposed to be jogging his memory," I said.

I got out of the car, told Styx to get in, and pulled Booster into a doorway.

"You got that gun?" I asked him.

"Search me."

160

He's only got this jacket on, and he opens it up. I don't see a gun. The Mouse feels a little foolish patting down a kid in a doorway, but I do it. Nothing.

"You learn fast, kid," I said.

We went back to the group.

"What was that all about?" Styx asked.

"Just a little secret between me and my man," I said.

"Let's coordinate our watches," Sam said when we got near the bank.

"I'm not wearing a watch," I said.

Beverly gives me a look like I'm stupid or something, but Sheri just giggles. I look to see if Styx is wearing a watch. He is.

Everybody with a watch coordinates their times. It was ten thirty-three and the "caper" was supposed to go off at ten forty.

"We do it just the way we talked it up," Sam said. "We go through the whole thing real casual like. Nobody talks to the kid. Soon as he remembers something he lets us know. If he remembers while he's in the bank, he gives us the signal and we walk right out. If he don't remember, he comes out and we take off down the street in the same way that he went with Katie and see if he can figure it out. Think hard, kid."

I wondered how come Sam was giving the orders when I was supposed to be in charge. Maybe because I didn't have a watch.

There wasn't a parking space in sight so Sam had to double-park in front of a truck that was delivering groceries to a small bodega.

"Slick, you want to sit in the car while I go in?" Sam asked.

"Yeah," Gramps said.

What he wanted to do was to motor that machine, not just sit in it.

"Who's going to be the lookouts?" Booster asked.

"Me and Beverly," Sheri said.

So off we go into the bank. I'm walking with Booster, and Sam and Styx are together. Booster's putting on this gimpy strut that I guessed was his version of how gangsters walked.

"Look, Booster, don't get carried away," I said. "You're supposed to be trying to remember something."

"If we find the money I'm spending mine on video games," Booster said.

"Yeah, well, just get your mind off the games right now and onto the cash," I said.

"Okay. Grandma and me walked into the bank," he said. "Grandma said that when she was with her real gang there was a guard over there where Sam and the big guy are standing."

"Styx. The big guy is Styx," I said.

"Then this guy that they were with went over and made believe he was tying his shoe while he checked things out."

"Go on," I said. "Make believe you're tying your shoe."

I watched as Booster went over near a potted plant, knelt, and pretended to tie his shoe. Then The Mouse's eyes did a double take and tried to jump out of his head. When Booster knelt and his pants leg came up I saw something silver sticking in his sweat socks. It was the gun!

I rushed across the floor and snatched it just as he pulled it out. Well, I almost snatched it. The gun went skidding across the marble floor and banged against an umbrella stand.

A heavyset lady saw me and Booster kneeling on the floor, looked at the gun, and started for the door.

"You ain't gettin' my money!" she hollered.

Booster made a break for the gun and I just managed to beat him to it with enough time to kick it across the floor. A couple of other people had seen the gun by this time and somebody screamed.

A woman and a tall black guy wearing a Yankees jacket started running toward the side door. I don't think they knew why they were running, just following the crowd. The guard heard the scream, saw them running, and tackled the guy in the Yankees jacket. The two of them slid along the floor and knocked over the potted plant.

"Sound the alarm! Sound the alarm!"

This was from the guy who was helping the guard hold down the guy in the Yankees jacket. A skinny lady had dropped a jar of dimes and held one hand over her head as she tried to scoop them up.

"It's my Christmas Club money!" She was trying to pull in some of the dimes with her foot.

I crawled over to the gun and picked it up. I didn't see anybody looking at me so I dropped it in the umbrella stand.

"The bank's being robbed! The bank's being robbed!" a teller was screaming.

"Yeah! Yeah!" Booster was shouting.

"No, that brother over there is robbing it," a black lady called out. She's pointing to where about four people are now sitting on the guy wearing the Yankees jacket.

"No, it's me!" Booster shouts out.

"Mouse! Let's split!" Styx was calling me.

164

"I got a gun, lady!" Booster is still yelling his head off. I've got his wrist and I'm trying to pull him away from the scene.

"*Gun!*"

People were diving for the floor. Booster was yelling. The woman that was with the guy in the Yankees jacket is trying to get them off of him. Only one guy is figuring Booster to be telling the truth. He starts over toward Booster and Sam sees him.

"Hey, Mister!"

The guy turns for just a minute and Sam decks him. Cold. Case closed.

"Booster has a gun!" I said to Sam.

"Where is it?" he asked.

"In the umbrella stand!" I said, steady scoping for the door.

A moment before everybody was running out of the bank. Now all of a sudden everybody is running into it. Three cops come in one door and they're jumping on the guy with the Yankees jacket. Two cops come in another door and they grab the lady scooping up the dimes.

Sheri comes in, too. She walks up to us real fast.

"Am I supposed to say anything for real if the cops come?"

I start toward the door and Booster grabs my

165

arm. I thought he was trying to hold me back but he's just taking my arm as we split.

There are a million people outside the bank and we have to fight our way through them to get to Gramps.

"What happened?" he asked.

"You seriously don't want to know," I said.

We waited for a second as Sam, carrying the umbrella stand, crossed the street and piled in the back on top of me and Booster and Styx got in the front with Gramps. Sheri and Beverly walked in the opposite direction down the street as Gramps wheeled the Packard away from the crowd.

"Please let me be dreaming!" Styx had his hand over his eyes. "Please don't let me be awake!"

"I got it! I remember!" Booster was saying. "Go one more block and turn right!"

13

Ka-Pow Da Dum Ka-Pow Da Dum!
Ka-Pow Da Dum Ka-Pow Da Dum!
When things get rough the crew gets tight
We run the stuff to make it right
We take the chances we got to take
We bend a little but we do not break
We work our show, we have our fun
We slide and glide till the job is done
Ka-Pow Da Dum Ka-Pow Da Dum!
Ka-Pow Da Dum Ka-Pow Da Dum!

☆

"You what!?"

I thought Gramps was going to explode as we sat at the stoplight.

"Slick, it was going to be a breeze but the kid messed it up," Sam said.

"And anyway it don't matter," Booster said. "I remember where Grandma took me."

"There's a police car behind us!" Styx said.

Gramps sat up quickly and looked in the rear-view mirror.

"Everybody stay loose," he said.

We sat stock-still. Nobody spoke. I had a vision of The Mouse breaking rocks on a chain gang.

"He's getting out of his car." Styx tried to slide down in his seat.

"Get up and act natural!" Gramps whispered.

I didn't want to turn around. I told my head not to move but my neck started turning and my head went along for the ride. I watched as the cop moved alongside his own car and then started slowly toward us. He stopped, looked at the back of the car, then came up toward Gramps' window.

"Nice car you have here, buddy." The policeman shook his head.

"They—they—don't make 'em like this anymore." Gramps tried to manage a grin.

"You think you can get it started?"

"I can get it started," Gramps said.

"Well, since the light changed about two minutes ago, why don't you try getting it started and be on your way?"

Gramps turned, looked at the light, and then looked back at the police officer.

"That light looks red to me, sir."

"It's red now, Pop," the officer said. "But it was green a little while ago. Look, it's green again."

Gramps turned and looked at the light again. It had turned back to green. The officer was smiling as we eased by him.

"Sam, I'm sorry I ever seen your ugly face again!" Gramps said, driving with one hand and banging on the dashboard with the other hand.

"Slick, at least we did something exciting," Sam said. "It sure beats sitting around the park."

"I'd rather sit around the park then be sitting in Alcatraz!"

"They closed Alcatraz," Sam said.

"They'd open it for a couple of old fools like us!" Gramps said.

"But I remembered where Grandma took me," Booster kept saying. "Just turn up this street and . . ."

Gramps didn't stop. He didn't stop until we had got back to Sheri's house. Then he let us all have it. He said that he had never been arrested

169

in all his life, and that he was too old to start a career as a jailbird.

We were all out on the sidewalk in front of Sheri's house and Gramps still didn't let up. We were attracting a small crowd. Sam was taking off his jacket getting ready to fight Gramps. Booster wasn't even interested. He had this real excited look on his face. Meanwhile, Sam and Gramps are getting ready to knock knuckles.

"Somebody stop them!" Sheri says.

We all jumped between them and tried to calm them down.

"What those men fighting about?" a woman called down from her window.

"They're both in love with me," Beverly said. "You know how *that* goes."

The woman gave Beverly a look that would have curdled ice water. I looked at Styx and he looked at me. Neither one of us thought it was that funny.

Gramps told Sam to take Booster home. "You so happy the little puppy knows how to pick pockets, maybe you can teach him something useful."

Later that day, after all my internal parts had slid down from my throat and settled into their regular places, I thought about how I handled everything. I mean, for my first bank job, I was pretty cool.

The evening news had a story about how the bank guard had foiled a robbery. They said he was a Vietnam war veteran and had spotted the robbery right away. He said if he hadn't fallen over a patron in a Yankees jacket he would have captured the would-be robbers. By the next day the papers were off our case and talking about an oil spill on the Jersey shore. The crew had had enough excitement for a while and everybody lay low for three days. I kept checking the papers for more stories about the bank, but there was nothing in them. In fact, the only thing that was in the paper at all was about a water shortage in Indiana.

It was the next Monday before we heard from Sam again. Sheri said he called Gramps three times and they argued over the phone each time. But eventually Sam made a breakthrough and got Gramps to go with him to check out the building where Booster said that his grandmother had taken him. One of Gramps' conditions was that Sam didn't bring Booster along.

What they found out was that the building had been condemned years before and now belonged to the city.

171

Sam, naturally, was all for breaking in and searching for the money, but Gramps didn't want any part of it and he made it clear that he wasn't going to let Sheri have any part in breaking into a building, either.

"He said that Sam and Booster and you could be criminals if you wanted to but his granddaughter was going to *be* something," Sheri said on the phone.

"How did The Mouse get hooked in there with the criminal element?" I asked her.

"I don't know," she said, laughing. "But I always thought you were a little shaky."

"Thanks, I needed that."

"So what are we going to do next?" Sheri asked.

"I don't know," I said. "But never fear, for The Mouse is here with his brain in gear. Can an answer be far away?"

She wasn't convinced. But that was okay. The more they doubt the more they shout when the Amazing Mouse has figured it out.

The next call was from the Booster himself.

"I guess I kind of messed things up the other day, huh?"

"Messed things up? No, Booster, you didn't mess things up, you just messed them around. If you had had a chance to do your thing you would have messed things up. But you didn't even get nobody killed. Nobody got maimed, or burned at the stake. Nobody got into jail either, but you came pretty close there, brother Booster."

"It's not going to happen again," he said. "I was thinking about it and everything and I really felt bad. I don't have a lot of friends and you guys are real nice. I'd just like to be like you."

"Hey, good thinking, man," I said. "That's really the way to go. Get a good education and you can make something of yourself like your grandmother wanted you to."

"Okay, Mouse, thanks a lot."

"No sweat, Booster," The Mouse said, digging the fact that the kid had joined the real world.

"And Mouse?"

"Yeah?"

"You think we really ought to have girls in our gang?"

☆

Okay, so The Mouse is laying out, stone to the world. The tape is tucked away. The magic tube is dark. Ma Bell is in the cradle. There's not a book open in my room. Everything is on Oh Double Eff. Then, *Bam!* The Mouse gets a serious flash! He sits right up in bed! Everything is solved in one glorious moment. I eased back down. I didn't want to shake my head and let it get loose, that's how heavy the flash was. The ideas were on a roll, The Mouse back in control.

Ceil ring-a-dings me a half hour later and says she's been sick.

"What you got?"

"I had the flu," she says. She sounds like she still has the flu. But I don't mention it.

"How you feeling now?"

"Okay in a way," she says. "But I feel bad about you."

Now I know I hadn't seen Ceil for a few days and everything, but I was surprised she was already feeling badly about not seeing The Mouse. In fact I was wondering if she had heard about me and Beverly and got sick behind that. You know, psychoflu-matic or something.

"Yo, that's the way it be's sometime," I said.

"You didn't have that much of a chance to practice and the contest is tomorrow. We going to practice tonight at ten, but my mother wants everybody there by nine thirty."

"I'll be there," I said.

The dance contest was part of The Mouse's big flash. If things worked out at the contest the way I hoped they would, the everything scale would hit the max mark and stay there.

174

When I got to Ceil's place I was ready to prance and dance. I was keeping time like a clock tick-tocking, I had my fingers snapping and my Reeboks rocking. I ran my show from head to toe, jumping in the air like Fred Astaire. When it came to learning I was the supergrad, and everybody said that The Mouse was BAD. Bring on the Games!

Okay, let me set the scene. We're in the park. Not just The Mouse and his crew but a thousand thousand people. There are dudes selling balloons, mamas with their kids, dogs wagging their tails, tails wagging their dogs, ants, uncles, winos, preachers, nuns, dudes in suits, dudes playing basketball, two ice cream trucks, cops, two vans from the television studios, three limousines, and one guy wearing a sign saying it was too late to repent. Picture all this commotion, then add forty-five million kids, each with a ball or a costume and trying to run to get to someplace before some other kid got there.

Did I tell you it was hot? Yo, like the sun came out and wanted to lay down the ground rules. You will sweat today! You will drink a lot of water! You will know that I am up here! Okay, so I could dig the heat.

I had Touch-Toned Booster early in the rise and he was on the scene. This time I searched the little sucker from head to toe and he was unarmed.

The program got started a half hour late with the handing out of some trophies. The team that had won the baseball tournament was there, and they picked up their trophies and smiled at the camera.

I parked Booster and scoped the scene for my favorite channel and they were there, and leading them was the woman who warmed the inside of the magic tube, Margie Davis. A smile pleased itself crawling across my face.

They were going to have the finals of the double Dutch tournament and then the talent contest.

Okay, so I dug the finals of the double Dutch tournament. Some kids from 116th Street won. They were really fine. We dished out some polite claps and then got on with the Main Event. The talent contest.

The first part of the talent tournament was singing groups. Some girl singers I had never seen before won one prize and some guys from the performing arts high school won one for the boys.

In the second part there was only one single dancer. That was a girl who did some ballet with a record playing, and nobody liked her that much. Then there were four dance groups. We were to be the last.

The first group didn't even do a dance. What they did was like a marching band number, but they still had some applause. Then The Mouse's stomach started acting funny.

"Yo, Styx, how you feel, man?"

"Like I should have been doing something else this morning," Styx said.

The second dance group was good. They did mostly fast stuff and they didn't do it together, but the girls were good-looking.

The next group did an African number and I thought they had won the whole thing because everybody clapped for them and the judges were shaking their heads and everything.

"Just think of yourselves as wonderful," Mrs. Bonilla said. "Because that's what you are. Wonderful."

Mr. Bonilla had this tape recorder set up and he started it. We started dancing and it felt pretty good, but I wasn't getting into it. Ceil was dancing great, but I could tell that sometimes she was adding things to the dance because I was a little bit behind her. Then something funny happened. Right in the middle of the dance we switch partners for a while. When we did that I was dancing with Sheri and Ceil was dancing with Omega. When they started dancing together it changed. The whole thing changed.

People started clapping for them and they were great. We were all supposed to be dancing in the middle, but me and Styx ended up dancing more to the side than in the middle. Somebody—I think it was Mrs. Bonilla—slowed the music down. Soon everybody was watching Ceil and Omega. It was half basketball and half something else. Flashes were going through The Mouse's mind so fast he could hardly keep up with them. The whole idea of Ceil's mama putting the basketball thing into the dance was heavier than I thought. And who should cop the program any better than Omega, the dude who was deepest into the moves? I definitely dug it.

Then it was all over and everybody was clapping. Two minutes later we found out we came in second.

Second. They put the kids who did the African dance in front of us. Sheri wanted to boohoo and Ceil was so messed around she went right to the hooing, she didn't even bother with a boo.

But The Mouse is on a mission. I'm checking

178

around to find out where Margie Davis is. Then I see her off to one side talking into the camera. I take a deep breath and slide on over until I'm close enough to the microphone to bite it. There I am standing in my costume and my no-cavs gleaming from ear to ear. Margie looks at me and gives me a smile.

"You kids had probably the most unusual dance of all," she says. Up close I can really see how cute her dimples are and my heart is pit-a-patting away like crazy. "Have you been interested in dance a long time?"

The microphone is aimed at The Mouse. Mission accomplished.

"No," I said. "But I'm interested now. It was the most interesting thing we did this summer, except for finding the money that other guy was looking for."

Now Margie doesn't know what I'm talking about. Only she's still smiling and the next thing I know I'm talking about how Gramps and Sudden Sam and Booster and us found the treasure but couldn't get into the building. Margie never stops smiling. Then she's thanking me and takes my name and she's gone on to talk to somebody else. Another guy from the station gets my address.

I check the time and it's only an hour since I

first walked into the park. I told everybody what I had said to Margie.

"What did she say?"

"She didn't exactly say anything," I said. "But she looked like . . . you know."

"She was smiling?" Sheri asked.

"Yeah."

"That's what she always does," they said.

No fear. Check out the news, right? The Mouse was not on the news. They showed fifteen seconds of the girls jumping double Dutch and then switched to the sports. Nothing.

Hurt. Pain. All that bad stuff was on The Mouse's pain button when Margie Davis, her precious dimpled self, called from the television station and asked Mom what I had meant when I had said that we had found the money. Mom tells them to talk to me and I ran the whole story down again. Meanwhile, Mr. D, who was sitting in The Mouse's favorite chair like he owned the sucker, is staring at me with his eyes bugged out as I'm running down how me and actual real live people from the Tiger Moran gang were looking for the treasure. Only I left out the bank part. Just in case.

Margie says okay in this real dead voice and tells me to stay by the phone. I hang up after kissing Ma Bell and I'm in the living room and I'm all excited. Mr. D starts shooting questions at Mom about if she knew what her son was doing and Mom says naturally she did, and she gives me a wink.

Then Margie calls me back and asks me to get everybody together and we're going to go treasure hunting with Channel 5, if it's all right with me. The Mouse says that it's all right, out of sight and pure delight.

Two days later we're crawling around in this old building and we spend thirty minutes on the first floor with this awful stink while the television crew figures out how they're going to get enough light to film the place. Beverly was checking out a cameraman and Sheri was mostly holding onto Gramps' arm while he grumbled. Booster had brought his mom along and was busy looking like one of those little angels with wings you see on old-time Christmas cards.

There was a guy there from the city, too. He just looked around like something was going to jump out and get him.

We went from floor to floor until we came to some offices called Moran's Moving and Storage. The guy from the city said that he didn't have the key and one of the cameramen tried the door,

181

gave it a nudge with his shoulder, and we were in.

The place was so damp and musty it was hard to breathe and one of the guys in the camera crew started sneezing.

We looked around for almost half an hour and didn't come up with anything but dustballs and some old newspapers. The camera guy who was sneezing started talking about how the whole idea was stupid and that we should leave. People were beginning to agree with him, too.

"Look, I think maybe we'll call it off," Margie said.

The camera crew started taking down their equipment as soon as the words got out of Margie's mouth.

"Leave enough light so that nobody gets hurt," the guy from the city said.

The cameraman had a belt with batteries on it and he took it off and placed it on top of an old desk, the kind where the front rolls down. He put one of the portable lights on it, too, while they got the rest of their gear together.

"Anybody look in that desk?" I asked.

"Nobody," the camera guy said. "Let's get out of here."

Styx went to the desk and tried to open it. It didn't come open.

"That's public property," the guy from the city said. "You can't damage it."

"Open it," Margie said.

Styx picked up a bar from the floor and put it under the rolltop.

I went over and gave Styx a hand. We pushed and one side of the desk went up, and then the whole thing popped open.

Margie had a flashlight. She went over and looked at the things on the desk.

"Can you guys get the drawers open?"

"We sure can," I said.

We could and did. There were two heavy doors that swung open and a lot of small drawers behind them. There wasn't much in most of them— some papers, a half bottle of whiskey, an old thermos bottle. No money.

"Some of these things have false bottoms and secret compartments," Margie said.

The cameraman groaned, and Margie shot him a dirty look.

We took all the drawers out and looked behind them. Nothing. Then there was a little knob on the side of the door that swung out and I pulled on that. The whole panel fell out.

And what fell out behind it was stacks of money. Stacks and *stacks* of money.

Okay, so that's the whole story. Just about. That night we were all on television, including The Mouse. The treasure turned out to be almost fifty thousand dollars in these old one-hundred-dollar bills. The Mayor said that the money officially belonged to the city but that he was going to recommend to the City Council that we be allowed to keep it. He said he might even turn the warehouse into housing for senior citizens.

You know what? Sam and Gramps didn't even care about the money. The most important thing to them was how everybody was coming around to get their story. They must have made a half dozen papers, including one all the way over in

London, England. Either they sit on the park bench across from my house or Gramps goes out to Queens where Sam lives and they tell people all about their gang days. And you know who's sitting right there listening to every word? Right. The Booster. I just hope he doesn't tell anybody about *his* bank-robbing days.

Omega, the great basketball player, got a dance scholarship to college. If I'm lying you know what else I'm doing. If I was sure he wouldn't break me in half I'd definitely crack on him about it.

Ceil is getting into more ballet, and I think she's going to be pretty good. Her moms is really proud.

Mr. D is still talking about getting his nest together and the moms person is still listening and I'm beginning to think she's really digging what she's hearing.

Styx started going out with Sheri but it's not like a colossal thing. They're just making it a light number. That left the Bev person for The Mouse and she has seen the error of her ways and begged The Mouse to be her friend.

Hey, The Mouse lives and he lets, he forgives and forgets. But when I fell into her crash she tells me she has bought a pet. Was it a tweet-tweet? A turtle with an American flag painted on his shell? No, man, it was a snake. A slither. A

185

creepy crawler. An asp. She said the sucker wasn't poisonous but it didn't make The Mouse no never mind. The Mouse does not like things that crawl on their belly and do not go woof-woof or tweet, my man, tweet. Nor could The Mouse dig himself in a lip lock with his eyes closed so he should not peep where the creep was creeping. Beverly and The Mouse were now History.

So once again The Mouse is Out Here On His Own. But hey, somebody has to stay loose and keep things under control, right?

☆

Chm Chm Chmmm, De De Deee
What's gotta be, gotta be-be-be
Don't run no jive, don't sing no blues
I just TCB and pay my dues
'Cause I'm the table topper, the stardust
    dropper
The neat Tip-Topper and the Fleet
    Hip-Hopper
You've heard my story, you've dug my show
You've rapped the rhythm and felt the flow
But now it's time for The Mouse to split
'Cause the tale is ended when the pieces fit
Chm Chm Chmmm, De De Deee
What's gotta be, gotta be-be-be
YES!